G. Linnaeus (George Linnaeus) Mrs. Banks, G. Linnaeus (George
Linnaeus) Banks

Daisies in the Grass

A Collection of songs and Poems

G. Linnaeus (George Linnaeus) Mrs. Banks, G. Linnaeus (George Linnaeus) Banks

Daisies in the Grass
A Collection of songs and Poems

ISBN/EAN: 9783744765442

Printed in Europe, USA, Canada, Australia, Japan

Cover: Foto ©Andreas Hilbeck / pixelio.de

More available books at **www.hansebooks.com**

DAISIES IN THE GRASS:

A Collection of Songs and Poems,

BY

MR. AND MRS.

G. LINNÆUS BANKS.

LONDON:

ROBERT HARDWICKE, 192, PICCADILLY, W.

———

1865.

LONDON:

PRINTED BY JOHN KING AND COMPANY, LIMITED,
QUEEN STREET, E.C.

TO

H. P.,

LOVER OF TRUTH, OF NATURE, AND OF HUMANITY,

This Volume

IS DEDICATED WITH DEEP RESPECT.

PREFACE.

Custom demands a Preface, and we, in all humility, bow to her behest.

There is little to be said, however, in issuing a work of this kind, save that we owe it to ourselves to state, in order to prevent any possible imputation of plagiarism or piracy, that the "Neglected Wife," and several other of the poems by Mrs. Banks, were published either in her own volume, "Ivy Leaves," or in current journals, while she was yet Isabella Varley; and that not a few of those by Mr. Banks, published in former volumes bearing his name, or in the magazines of the day, have been appropriated in various quarters without his authority, and in some cases actually endorsed by initials or *sobriquets* wholly strange to him.

In instances where the sister art, Music, has been called into request, the names of composers and publishers are given, in common fairness to both.

33, CLOUDESLEY SQUARE, N.,

June 30*th*, 1865.

" The daisies in the grass are singing."

—HERAUD'S "*Angel of the Ages.*"

CONTENTS.

	PAGE.
THE VOLUNTEERS' BATTLE CALL	13
TWO HEROES AND TWO GRAVES	17
WHAT I LIVE FOR	21
RETURNS	24
HERE'S TO THE SAXON! AND HERE'S TO THE DANE!	26
THE TRIED AND TRUE	29
REMEMBERED TONES	31
THE HEAVENLY CHORISTER	32
THE LESSON OF THE LEAVES	34
DAY IS BREAKING	36
THE GOOD SPIRIT	39
THE KING OF THOUGHT	41
PRAYEST THOU?	45
MRS. BROWN AND MRS. GREEN	51
HELICON UNDER A CLOUD	55
THE WORKMAN AND HIS WORK	59
THY VOICE IS NOW SILENT	64
MINE!	65
THE DEAD CHIEF	67
MIDNIGHT BY THE SEA	69
DECEIVED	71
MAKE WAY	72
DREAMS OF AN ENTHUSIAST	78
OUT IN THE WORLD	86
THE ABSENT ONE	89
A HOME SONG FOR HOME BIRDS	90
LABOUR'S FESTIVAL	91
A BEGGAR'S PETITION	95
SABBATH ASPIRATIONS	97
THE LEAF AND THE SOUL	101
TO MY WIFE	103
MY HOME IS ON THE MOUNTAIN STEEP	105
THE SEEN AND UNSEEN	107
SONGS OF THE SEASONS	109

	PAGE.
THE NEGLECTED WIFE	116
CALCRAFT'S CARNIVAL	122
THE DISH WITH A COVER	126
O, BARD OF GENTLE AVON!	129
JOHN BULL AND THE GALLIC COCK	132
WINTRY HOURS	134
NEVERMORE, EVERMORE	135
GOOD WE MIGHT DO	138
A MOTHER'S VOICE	140
THE HAUNTED TOWER	142
SERVICES AND REWARDS	145
WOULD'ST THOU BE A CHILD AGAIN?	149
A WORD FOR THE WORKERS	155
THE MINSTREL OLD AND GREY	157
THE GIPSY GIRL	159
UNREAD LESSONS	161
THE STATE PILOT	163
LABOUR'S PROGRESS AND TRIUMPH	165
THE THREE BLACK D's.	170
THE QUIET JOYS OF HOME	173
DESOLATION	175
BETTER THINGS SHALL COME TO PASS	177
PARTING WORDS	181
THE MEN OF OLD	183
HOUSEHOLD TREASURES	185
JOAN D'ARC	187
SLANDER!	191
MY DEAD BABE'S HAIR	199
ROUND AND ROUND THE CORAL BOWER	201
THE GOLDEN CALF	203
FANNY'S VALENTINE	205
LION-HEARTED ENGLAND	207

THE VOLUNTEERS' BATTLE CALL.

(1859.)

Sons of the old heroic dead
   Whose deeds, embalmed in story,
Tell of a nation's life-blood shed
   To form a nation's glory !
Hear ye yon distant thunder peal ?
   War's footsteps onward creeping ;
Mark ye the flash of fire and steel,
   Through yon dark cloudlet peeping ?
Sure as the dawn precedes the day,
That war-cloud rolls along our way,

B

And English guns and English men
In fire must roll it back again!

    Up! for your lives, with blade and brand,
    Shoulder to shoulder, hand to hand,
    A living wall of valour stand,
    In name of God and Fatherland!

Sons of the chiefs who won this land
    Of old with crimson'd sabre!
Sons of the elder, mightier band—
    The ancient chiefs of labour!
The pride of birth, the pride of toil,
    Both feed the patriot spirit,
And both shall slumber in the soil
    Or e'er they disinherit
Our brave old country of the place
She's gain'd by strength of arm and race,
And still shall keep, though tempests roar,
And waves despotic lash her shore!

    Up! for your lives, with blade and brand,
    Shoulder to shoulder, hand to hand,
    A living wall of valour stand
    In name of God and Fatherland!

Sons of the old storm-beaten kings
   Whose empire was the ocean ;
Whose memory, like an anthem, rings
   On lips of pure devotion !
Ye have not lost the Saxon nerve
   That brought us victory ever :
When was a Briton known to swerve ?
   Old Ocean answers, " Never !"
Long hath our glory swept the seas,
Free as the curbless mountain breeze ;
Come death, come ruin, ere the foe
Shall lay our sea-born glory low !

     Up ! for your lives, with blade and brand,
     Shoulder to shoulder, hand to hand,
     A living wall of valour stand
     In name of God and Fatherland !

Sons of the brave !   The foe assumes
   Our ancient strength departed,
He'd carve a million soldiers' tombs
   To own us lion-hearted ;
For come when will the bloody day
   That lights the fires of battle,

We'll meet his legions in the fray
   And drive them back like cattle ;
As would have done, in former years,
The band of British Volunteers,
But Heaven reserved for our great need
Th' immortal glory of the deed !

    Up ! for your lives, with blade and brand,
    Shoulder to shoulder, hand to hand,
    A living wall of valour stand
    In name of God and Fatherland !

                       G. L. B.

TWO HEROES AND TWO GRAVES.

(A TRIBUTE TO RICHARD COBDEN.)

OVER the field of Waterloo,
    Where banners wave, and sabres flash,
    And trumpets peal, and cymbals clash,
    And chargers neigh, as on they crash
Over the living, and over the slain,
    Trampling out life, and trampling down grain,
'Mid carnage and smoke, and demoniac fire
(Life's blood and life's food alike trod in the mire),
    Gallops a hero to dare and do.
        The fight is fought, a battle won,
        Between the rise and set of sun;
        And thousands weep when all is done;

Some o'er the dying, and some o'er the dead,
And some o'er the fall of a crownéd head.
But Wellington comes with the wreath he has won,
And England honours her Warrior Son
    As the best of her brave and true.

Over the site of Peterloo,
    (Marked by a scene from which we shrink,
    Where mounted yeomen, fired with drink,
    Sabred people who dared to think ;
Cutting down women, and firing on men,
Reckless of right for the tongue or the pen).
In a plain broad structure new battles are planned,
To *Free* from restrictions the *Trade* of the land,
    The fetters on commerce undo !
        Thought and speech are the weapons *there*,
        With earnest will and genius rare ;
        And thousands troop the fight to share :
    That marvellous army by Cobden led,
    To wrest from Protection the people's bread.
But smiles, not tears, mark his victory's track;
And millions unborn shall yet look back
    On *this* Hero, the tried and true !

Under the great cathedral dome
   Men are marching with arméd heel,
   Solemn step, and the clink of steel,
   Drowned by the deep bell's muffled peal,
And the anthem swelling throughout the pile,
O'er marble heroes in chancel or aisle,
O'er the sailor who lies in the vaults below,
O'er the corse of the soldier, so soon to go
   To his rest in that stately tomb,
   With catafalque and sable pall,
   Trappings of woe on steeds,—and all
   That mourns the great—*become so small.*
And the Iron Duke is buried in state,
   In the heart of the city, noisy and great ;
With pageant and pomp from his chosen retreat,
On a funeral car through the crowded street,
   Borne to his grand sepulchral home.

On the slope of a Sussex hill,
   Where the dews of heaven may fall
   Like the tears rained over his pall,
   In the rest which awaits us all,
Lies the Hero who fought a bloodless fight,
In the war with wrong for a nation's right.

And a people's sorrow has followed him there:
They. mourn for the man who their sorrows could share,
   For the warm heart quiet and chill.
     Friends and kindred over him weep,
     Statesmen grieve for the mind asleep,
     The church-bell sobs its echo deep,
   Tolling for one who has passed from the strife,
   Marshalled by Death through the portals of Life,
Has fought a good fight, and the victory won.
Christian and Patriot thou hast " well done,"
   And Peace smoothes thy bed on the hill!

ISAB B.

WHAT I LIVE FOR.

I LIVE for those who love me,
  Whose hearts are kind and true;
For the Heaven that smiles above me,
  And awaits my spirit too;
For all human ties that bind me,
For the task by God assigned me,
For the bright hopes yet to find me,
  And the good that I can do.

I live to learn their story
  Who suffered for my sake;
To emulate their glory,
  And follow in their wake:

Bards, patriots, martyrs, sages,
The heroic of all ages,
Whose deeds crowd History's pages,
    And Time's great volume make.

I live to hold communion
    With all that is divine,
To feel there is a union
    'Twixt Nature's heart and mine ;
To profit by affliction,
Reap truth from fields of fiction,
Grow wiser from conviction,
    And fulfil God's grand design.

I live to hail that season
    By gifted ones foretold,
When men shall live by reason,
    And not alone by gold,
When man to man united,
And every wrong thing righted,
The whole world shall be lighted
    As Eden was of old.

I live for those who love me,

    For those who know me true,

For the Heaven that smiles above me,

    And awaits my spirit too ;

For the cause that lacks assistance,

For the wrong that needs resistance,

For the future in the distance,

    And the good that I can do.

G. L. B.

RETURNS.

―――

"Is not thy rest the offspring of thy toil?
Is not thy labour pole of thy repose?"

MACKAY'S EGERIA.

―――

"FROM the gay world, with all its gilded troubles,
Its phantom pleasures, and its bursting bubbles;
Worn with its tumult and its wild unrest,
Back like a fledgling to the parent nest,

Mother, I come, I come,

To childhood's quiet home,
To lay my aching head once more upon thy breast."
" Welcome, my son, thou truant long estranged;
Welcome to home and heart, both peaceful and unchanged

From my pure home, the loveable and quiet,

ack to the city's din, if not its riot;

rom the repose for which I am unfitted

y all that has transpired since home I quitted,

   Mother, once more I go,

   With *work* to chase the woe

o closely by the Past in Life's web knitted."

Then go, my son, from scenes for thee too calm :

:epose for thee is poison, *labour* is sorrow's balm ! "

       Isab. B.

HERE'S TO THE SAXON! AND HERE'S
TO THE DANE!*

—— ——

PRINCE OF WALES' BRIDAL CHORUS FOR FOUR VOICES.

——

COME fill up a cup of the good Rhein wine,
    And we will a bumper drain
To the health of the Prince, and the Bride benign
    Who comes from the land of the Dane;
He's noble and free as the isle of his birth—
    She's gentle, and graceful, and fair—
O, search where you will through the length of the ea
    You'll find none with them can compare!

* Music by W. WILSON; published by METZLER & Co., Great
Marlborough Street, W.

Then here's to the Saxon! and here's to the Dane!
May the peaceful alliance unbroken remain,
And their thrones and their peoples, united and free,
Stand together as firm as a rock in the sea!

In centuries past when this good green sward
    Was tilled by the Saxon's hand,
The Viking came, and with fire and sword
    He ravaged our native land;
But a thousand years of toil and pain
    Have worked such wondrous spells,
Now, kings of the sea, we welcome the Dane
    With the music of marriage bells.

Then here's to the Saxon! and here's to the Dane!
May the peaceful alliance unbroken remain,
And their thrones and their peoples, united and free,
Stand together as firm as a rock in the sea!

All hail! to the Prince and Princess, blest
    With the joy such union brings—
When the love that glows in the peasant's breast
    Burns bright in the hearts of kings;

For wisest still is the grand old plan
    Which Nature herself lays down—
That queens should wed for the sake of the man,
    And not for the sake of the crown.

    Then here's to the Saxon! and here's to the Dane
    May the peaceful alliance unbroken remain,
    And their thrones and their peoples, united and fre
    Stand together as firm as a rock in the sea!

                 G. L. B.

THE TRIED AND TRUE

———

I PASS unregarded the selfish and vain,
  Who proffer a favour and make it a debt ;
For service so rendered comes loaded with pain,
  But true-hearted kindness I cannot forget.

From the butterfly friends, who, when summer was bright,
  Fluttered round me with offers I did not require ;
I turn to the few who in winter's dark night
  Were true and devoted—gold tried in the fire.

Or when prostrate in sickness, disabled by pain,
  Surrounded by hirelings, unheeded I lay ;
From paraded assistance I turn with disdain,
  But the true-hearted kind ones I ne'er can repay.

To these and these only will memory cling,
    For sympathy shown in look, action, or word ;
And the waters of gratitude ever upspring
    In the heart's brimming fount, though they sparkle unheard

The hand of the spoiler hath often been laid
    On the dear ones whose loss I must ever regret;
But the true friends I tried in those seasons of shade,
    Are embalmed in a heart which can *never* forget.

                                        ISAB. B.

REMEMBERED TONES.

I HEARD a sweeter voice last night
  Than I have heard for many a day,
Attuned to melody as light
  As zephyr's breath, or fairy lay ;
It seemed to tell of life's young spring
  Unshadowed by the clouds of time,
When love, and hope, and everything
  Went sweetly as a matin chime.

Mine ear, perchance, may never more
  Be captive led by that dear tone—
Ne'er run again its numbers o'er
  In sweet felicity alone ;
Yet, like the perfume of the May,
  That lingers tho' the May depart,
That gentle song for many a day,
  Shall wake an echo in my heart.

G. L. B.

c 2

THE HEAVENLY CHORISTER.

I HAVE a child in Heaven,
    Singing with perfect face before the Throne ;
Our God by whom 'twas given,
    Missed from the angel quire that dear one's tone,
And longing for it, with a Father's pride,
Called back the little wanderer to his side.

Placid his brow and fair
    When the swift-winged messenger drew near,
And my heart groaned a prayer,
    Which e'en Death shuddered, while he smote, to hear,
And half relented, when the work was done,
    To see my arms still clinging to my son.

I have a child in Heaven,

    Singing with radiant face at God's right hand,

And when life's closing even'

    Fades out upon the verge of that bright land,

My angel-boy shall leave the shining quire

To fling his arms about his earthly sire.

G. L. B

THE LESSON OF THE LEAVES.

GLANCING in the sunlight,
Dancing in the breeze,
See the new-born leaflets
On the summer trees :
Joying in existence,
Whisperingly they play,
Toying with each other
Through the golden day :
And when evening's eyelids
Close upon the hill,
Casting loving glances
On the answering rill :
Thus they dance and flutter
    All the summer through,
Light, and gay, and gladsome,
    Leaflets green and new :
" Life is all before us—life is full of glee ! "
Is the joyous chorus heard from every tree.

Hanging on the branches,
Drooping in the shade,
Mark the autumn leaflets
How they pine and fade ;
Rustling—as the storm-blast
Sweeps across the moor—
Driven by the whirlwind
To the cottar's door ;
Dark, and thick, and heavy,
With the dust of Time,
Weary of existence,
List their wintry chime,
As the mournful cadence
   Rings in human ears,
A never-ending moral
   For the coming years.
This the parting chorus—" Leaves, our course is run ;
Death is now before us—but *our work is done!* "

                           ISAB. B.

DAY IS BREAKING.

(A SONG OF PROGRESS)

DAY is breaking
On the mountain-tops of Time,
　As they stand head-bared and hoary,
Watching from their heights sublime
The new Morning upward climb
　In its creative glory!

Day is breaking,
Like a firmament of light　-
　Flushing far the heaving ocean;
And the darkness of the Night
Melts before its gathering might
　As a spectral thing in motion!

Day is breaking!
In the valleys, on the hills,
   The earth is as an infant swathed in brightness ;
And the rivers and the rills
With a sparkling joy it fills,
   As to lyric measure turns their rippling lightness !

Day is breaking!
And the matin of each bird—
   A ray of morn distilled in music—ringing
Through the welkin far, is heard
Echoing, like the parting word
   Of a lover to his earthly idol clinging!

Day is breaking,
Like a host of angels sent
   With some new revelation,
And the mourning nations bent,
Tiptoe wait the grand event—
   The mind's emancipation.

Day is breaking!
And from the grave of other years
  In new birth Life awaking,
Above the dust of Death uprears
Its face, no longer wet with tears,
  For mankind's Day is breaking.

Day is breaking!
And as the story of its advent flies,
  In the mart, on 'Change,
Sagacious men, far-seeing, questioning, wise,
Tarry to fathom in each other's eyes
  The import deep and strange.
    Day is breaking!
A crimson rust feeds on the sword—
  Devoured by blood of its own shedding;
And where the cannon thundering roared,
To nobler peace and self restored,
  Man by the Light of God is treading.

G. L. B.

THE GOOD SPIRIT.

———

Of all the Good Spirits that brighten the earth
  Good Temper is surely the best,
And luckless the hearth where she's seldom at home,
  'Or comes but a casual guest ;
Where the plumage is torn from her delicate wings,
And little is thought of the blessings she brings.

Good Temper can give to the lowliest cot
  A charm with the palace to vie,
For gloomy and dark is the loftiest dome
  Unlit by her radiant eye ;
And 'tis she who alone makes the banquet divine,
Gives for viands ambrosia, and nectar for wine.

The world would be dreary and barren indeed,
   Our pilgrimage weary and sad,
Did the strife-seeking spirit of Sullenness reign,
   To trample on hearts that were glad;
He would blot out life's sunshine, and pluck up its flowers,
Driving Hope's sweetest song-birds away from its bowers.

Alas! that we ever should fall 'neath a sway
   So tyrannous, cruel, and stern—
Should wilfully chase fair Good Temper away,
   Her favours indignantly spurn;
For with her there is pleasure, and gladness, and light,
With Sullenness discord, and sadness, and night.

Let who will give the demon a place in his breast,
   May Good Temper preside over mine;
She will lighten my sorrows, and whisper to Care
   Fewer thorns in my chaplet to twine.
Then, be mine this Good Spirit, who comes at our call,
And would come, were she welcome, to each and to all.

ISAB. B.

THE KING OF THOUGHT.

An Address, written for the Performance, at Drury Lane Theatre, in aid of the " People's Shakespeare Memorial Fund," and delivered by Mr. Edmund Phelps, December 15th, 1864.

COULD these dumb Boards, instinctive with the tread
Of Mighty feet, speak of the Mightier Dead ;
Or these Old Walls the gift of speech attain,
My task were needless, and my presence vain ;
But sith they're silent, and the Human must
Still chronicle the Human in the dust,
I come, in humble service and respect,
To tell the story of our land's neglect.

There is a King all human Kings above,
Who rules unseen, in wisdom and in love—
Sits on a Throne of Stars, and in its light,
Woos the world's thought towards the Infinite :
No liveried placeman ambles in his court—
No crafty counsels of his will make sport—
No braggart chief, no hapless captive waits
Trembling and pale without his city gates ;
But ever as he sees the tyrant, Man,
Oppress the weak—so mar the Eternal plan—
Or poor Humanity go halting by,
Stricken with grief or sad infirmity ;
Moved by the deep Divinity within,
That speaks of all men as one kith and kin,
He grasps his suffering brother by the palm,
And nerves his soul with some life-giving psalm.

Who is this King of Kings ?   A voice replies,
Like a faint whisper of the midnight skies,
Telling of One who by the power of God,
Strangely endowed, rose from his native sod,
Near Avon's stream, to occupy a Throne,
In an ideal Empire of his own.

From out the Universe—the sea, earth, air—
His realm he peopled ; shapes as strange as fair
Came at his bidding, and, that none should die,
He wreathed their brows with Immortality.

Ages have flown and States decayed since then,
But no corruption taints his Sovereign Pen :
What He, the Master-limner, once hath traced—
What He, the Priest, upon the altar placed—
What He, the Prophet, hath proclaimed on high—
What He, the Poet, sung in rhapsody ;
His words, his thoughts, the music of his heart—
Of Nature's subtler self the subtler part—
Shall live, and breathe, and burn, till Time and Sense
Close their account 'twixt Man and Providence.

King for all time !   Where, then, the homage due
To Potentate so rare, so wise, so true ?
When was it paid ?   Where is it to be found ?
Alas ! not on one spot of English ground !
To bigots, butchers, despots, trophies stand
On many an acre of our smiling land,

But not to Him, whose letters-patent bore
The signet-seal of Heaven for evermore !

Be't ours to check this love of low-born things,
And slake the soul's deep thirst at purer springs !
Give WILL a Shrine in some befitting place,
Where, in the fair proportions of his face,
England, the one bright Island of the Sea—
Home of the Brave, and Birthplace of the Free—
May proudly show her reverence for the Pen,
And own the King of Thought the King of Men !

G. L. B.

PRAYEST THOU?

———

What! "*never prayed?*" Oh, say not so,—
    Thou canst not look around
Upon the God-blessed earth nor feel
    Thy every heart-pulse bound,
In gratitude and thankfulness
    To that Almighty Power
Whose name is writ in rainbow gems
    Upon the sunlit shower,—
In moonbeams on the light-kissed wave,
    Where stars reflected lie,
Like angel-eyes embroidered on
    Some heaven-wrought tapestry,—

D

Emblazoned on the verdant turf,
  In ever-springing flowers,
And hymned by birds, in gushing notes,
  Mid dim-arched forest bowers.

Come forth, then, thou who "never prayed,"
  Come forth in thought with me;—
We'll dive together to the depths
  Of the resounding sea;
Its labyrinthine caverns search,
  Each crystalline recess;—
Dost thou not feel 'mong Ocean's caves
  Thy puny littleness?
Millions of insect architects
  The coral-reef outspread,
And raise their island silently
  Where man in time may tread;
The busy waters teem with life,
  To grace his banquet board,
And pearls and gems for Beauty's brow
  Its lowest depths afford.

Come forth into the upper air,
    Where insect myriads swarm,
To vivify the atmosphere
    We breathe so fresh and warm.
The bee, arrayed in velvet vest,
    In quest of his sweet spoil,
For man, from morn till night, pursues
    His unremitting toil.
The bright-hued warbler, soaring far
    On beam-enamelled wings,
To gratify his eye and ear,
    Thus flutters, shines, and sings.
There, pierced by arrow, feather poised,
    From Indian bow-string sped,
For food or ornament required,
    A gay-plumed bird is dead.

Descend into the gloomy mines,—
    Say, what dost thou behold ?
Veins of bright metal intersect
    The wealthy earth's dark mould

Here lies the radiant diamond,—
   There virgin silver shines;
But Heaven bestows a better gift,—
   Our coal and iron mines.
Pile up coals upon the furnace,
   And fuse the iron ore!
The miner asks for implements
   Earth's secrets to explore;
The peasant needs the spade and plough
   To turn the yielding soil,—
The sickle and the scythe, to reap
   The harvest of his toil.   '

Ascend with me the mountain's height,
   Look forth upon the skies,—
Behold the laughing sunbeams play
   In infant Morning's eyes.
Like silver threads, the sparkling rills
   Dance merrily along,
And clasp each other's wavy arms
   With a rejoicing song;

United indissolubly,
 They fertilize the plain,
Invigorate the sapling's root,
 And swell the rising grain.
There, sheep are out upon the hills,
 Here bloom the dark-tressed vines ;
The pomegranate is deeply flushed,
 The autumn fruitage shines.

Come down into the vale again,
 Look forth into the world,
Before thine eyes on every side
 Are pleasant scenes unfurled.
Look to thine own domestic hearth,
 The friends assembled there,
And own that thou hast ample cause
 For thankfulness and prayer.
Look into thine own bosom's depths,—
 Thou hast a heart to feel :
Stifle not feelings as they rise,
 Thy closed lip unseal,

Thine is an intellect and mind
          To grasp the beautiful,—
How canst thou view the Lord's great works
          And not feel prayerful?

Thou hast prayed! yes, I know thou hast,
          And fervently and well;
Though thy hushed lips have breathed no tone—
          No words arise to tell
When thy full heart appeals to God
          In eloquence and prayer,
And prostrate at his footstool lays
          Its purest offering there.
I know, I feel, thy *heart* ascends
          In praise to Him e'en now,
Although thy *voice* may not respond
          To the soul-uttered vow.
Oh, no! thou art not—canst not be
          So lost in sin's black shade!—
'Twould madden me were I to think
          That thou hadst " NEVER PRAYED !"

                              . ISAB. B.

MRS. BROWN AND MRS. GREEN.

——

A VERY *fair* Christian is good Mrs. Brown,
And wise, too, as any in any wise town;
She worships her God without any display,
Not molesting her friend who lives over the way;
And, whatever occurs it is easy to see
That her words and her conduct do always agree.
For this little maxim she shrewdly commends—
" Good precept and practice should ever be friends ! "

A very *warm* Christian is good Mrs. Green,
In her satins, and velvets, and rich armazine;
She is always at church when the service begins,
And prays quite aloud for' the *poor* and their *sins;*
Then her speech is so fair, and her manner so bland,
They'd proselytise the most heathenish land;

And this one opinion she stoutly defends —
" That precept and practice should ever be friends ! "

Mrs. Brown has a reticule, useful though small,
Which oft in the week she takes under her shawl,
Calling first on this person, and then on the other,
As if she were either a sister or mother ;
And 't has often been remarked, with good reason, no doubt,
That the reticule's lighter for having been out ;
For this little maxim she shrewdly commends—
" Good precept and practice should ever be friends ! "

Mrs. Green, now and then, for an hour, sits in state
With some more lady friends—rich, of course—to debate
How the poor shall be clothed, and *what* taught, and *what*
        rules
It were best to enforce in the Charity Schools ;
All of which having over and over been turned,
And, nothing decided, the meeting's adjourned ;
And this one opinion each lady defends—
" That precept and practice should ever be friends ! "

In the street where resides our good friend Mrs. Brown
Is a school, though not known to a tithe of the town,

Which that lady supports from her own private purse;

(And 'tis thought by her neighbours she might do much
    worse;)

And if scholars, or parents, are ill or distressed,

The reticule's sure to be had in request;

For this little maxim she shrewdly commends—

" Good precept and practice should ever be friends ! "

Mrs. Green has a sympathy deep and refined,

It is not to parish or country confined;

If a party of ladies propose a bazaar

To enlighten the natives of rude Zanzebar,

She is truly delighted to sanction their aim,

By *giving* wise counsel, and *lending* her name;

For this one opinion she stoutly defends—

" That precept and practice should ever be friends ! "

Mrs. Brown is a stranger to parties and sects,

The good of *all* classes she loves and respects;

Thinking little enough of profession or creed,

If the heart and the hand go not with it indeed;

While her prayers, and her purse, and her reticule, too,

For *all* sorts of Christians a kindness will do;

And this little maxim she shrewdly commends—
"Good precept and practice should ever be friends!"

There are *few* Mrs. Browns—*not* a few Mrs. Greens,
In their satins, and velvets, and rich armazines.
There are *thousands* who'll preach, lend their names, and
      give rules,
But how *few* are provided with small reticules!
With the world, Mrs. Green, as a saint, will go down—
We will stake our existence on good Mrs. Brown,
Who in word, and in deed, the trite maxim commends—
"Good precept and practice should ever be friends!"

G. L. B.

HELICON UNDER A CLOUD.

———

On, Poetry! thou once wert like a rill
Rippling o'er pebbles; swelling to a stream
Strong, deep, and clear, a river between banks
Fringed with rank reeds or drooping willow-boughs;
Laving the gnarled roots of aged oaks
Or silvery birches—music in thy flow;
Thy lucent length a mirror for the moon
And all her midnight train of minstrel stars;
Or, when the day was gorgeous with the glow
Of fervid noon, the canopy o'erhead
On thy broad flood shone like a second sky;
And in thy limpid depths each living thing
Lightly disporting through its little life
With flashing fin, or coiling worm-like ring,

Or insect antennæ—each tuft of moss,
Each veiny pebble, every tiny weed,
Or skeleton of leaf which once was green
And dancing in the sun, was visible
To the observant eye.   The rudest hind,
The keen philosopher, might scan thy stream
Wiser and better for the scrutiny ;
Or childhood quench its thirst in the clear flood,
Which murmured sweetly truths to great and small.

Now, Poetry is like a turgid tide
Floating through crystal caverns, or deep hid
In gloomy mountain gorges, chafing here
O'er rocks and boulders in its rapid flight ;
Now flashing into light for a brief space
Under the sunny heavens ; sweeping soon
O'er jutting crags—a cataract of foam :
Whirling in eddies ere it settles down
Into its course—a sullen, sonorous stream,
Deep, strong, and dark, a tide without an ebb ;
The heavy umbrage of the forest trees
Shutting the sunlight out.   Sweet rivulets,
Fostered 'mid flowers, and singing with the birds,

May lose their way, and stray to the deep stream ;
Or snow-flakes melt their crystals in its flood,
To swell its waters and be seen no more,
As dew-drops seek the sun.   But on and on,
With a sad, surging sound, solemn and dark,
The waves of poetry still roll, and roll,
Too deep and mystic for the common ken.
What untaught foot may tread the wilderness,
To bathe within the stream, or climb the heights,
To search if light illume its secret source?
What eye, not lit by spiritual rays,
May penetrate the gloom that shades the stream,
Or pierce the night-black waters in their bed,
Or torch-like, light the cavern's crystals up ?

Thou grand majestic stream ! still keep thy course,
Swelling and deepening in the track of time ;
Shroud thy great beauty in mysterious woods,
Or deep ravines where daylight's self is dim—
Where only feet, with learned sandals shod,
May wander by thy side, or stand secure,
Whilst filtering through the transcendental brain
Thy living waters show their golden sands !

But turn aside at times into the meads ;
Court the broad sunshine—ripple in its beams,
Gilding thy breast with glory.   Glance and play
Like a coquette with fern and meadow-sweet ;
Let the swift swallow dip his travelled wing,
Or homely robin wash his scarlet vest,
And sip his morning draught.   Be clear once more ;
Come forth into the light !—Be Poetry—
A flood for all who choose to stoop and drink ;
Not a deep fount of metaphysic lore
Sealed up from half the world !

                                        ISAB. B.

THE WORKMAN AND HIS WORK.

———

THERE were twenty-six
   Black slender objects lay
Spread out before a toiling man,
   Each like a cast-away—
Unlike, and yet of kin they were;
   Apart, yet side by side;
Some round, some square, hump-backed and crossed—
   Others with legs bestride.
But O! their power was wond'rous great—
   How great scarce any knew—
For, though a child might use it well,
   No King could it subdue.

There were twenty-six,
    And he who turned them o'er,
But laboured at a daily task
    Oft laboured at before—
A two-fold recompence he sought,
    For fortune had not shed
Her glittering treasures round his heart,
    Her honours round his head—
So toiled he on, the livelong day,
    With weary touch and look ;
Until his work was done—and lo !
    Behold it made a *Book*.

A Book—a mighty Book—
    In which were glorious things
Bright words to warm the beggar's soul,
    And pierce the hearts of kings
Truths that, like polished crystals shone,
    And powerful made the weak—
That crimsoned deep with self-respect
    The wretched outcast's cheek—
No grandeur, beauty, might, or good
    Hath traversed earth around,

But in that white yet crowded page
   Its antetype was found.

It taught the pampered heir
   Humility, not state ;
And Dives, rich, to share his meal
   With beggars at his gate ;
The tyrant to relax the chain
   That brutalised the slave—
It furnished bright examples for
   The virtuous and brave.
It preached the death of bloody wars—
   It spoke, as can the Pen ;
And GOD, whose stamp it bore, looked down,
   And closed it with AMEN.

The man of toil went home,
   And sat beside his fire,
While little laughing children came
   And kissed their welcome sire—
No pomp, no splendour, hoarded up
   There, flashed upon his gaze ;

E

No cringing vassals, bowing down,
  Extolled with artful praise.
He was a poor, a working man,
  Obscure, and meanly clad,
With many cares to vex his soul,
  Nor much to make it glad.

The book—*that* Book—went forth,
  With an Almighty spell,
Politics tottered at his voice,
  And thrones before it fell—
The ocean bore its tidings on,
  To farthest clime and shore ;
And scattered holy gifts around,
  Where none had been before.
Where'er it went, the human mind
  A glorious thing became—
The Indian and the African
  Put on a God-like name.
Men—sceptics—soon stepped forth,
  And, with unholy mirth,
Essayed to make that mighty Book
  A blank throughout the earth—

In library and cloistered cell,
   With skill and zeal uprose,
Philosopher and saintly monk,
   Its charmed leaves to close—
The sword and rack in turn were tried,
   And every desperate plan,
But nothing could undo the work
   Of that poor toiling man.

The Workman died —unsung, unknown ;
   But soon, by heaven's light,
His spirit gazed in glory down
   Upon our mortal night—
A mighty change the Book had wrought ;
   War, lust, and wrong, and pride
Were smitten, and a better fruit
   Was ripening far and wide—
Whose small seeds, scattered by his hand
   Upon the human sod,
Should stock the Paradise above
   With flowers approved by God !

G. L. B

F 2

THY VOICE IS NOW SILENT.

Thy voice is now silent, the hearth is now cold,
Where thy smile and thy welcome oft met me of old;
I miss thee and mourn thee, in silence, unseen—
I dwell on the memory of joys that have been;
But nor weeping, nor memory affords me relief,
For my heart is bowed down with the weight of its grief.

I know that life's sorrows with thee are all past,
That thy spirit with angels is happy at last,
For in dreams of the night, when the world is at rest,
I list to thee singing the songs of the blest;
But those moments, so blissful, are restless and brief,
And my heart is bowed down with the weight of its grief.

G. L. B.

MINE!

"A WIFE'S SONG."

I LOVE thee, I love thee, as dearly as when
    We plighted our troth in the spring-time of life;
,The tempests of years have swept o'er us since then,
    Yet affection survives both in Husband and Wife.

No love that the poet ere fabled of yore
    Could vie in its depth or endurance with mine;
No miser could treasure his glittering store
    As I hoard in my heart every love-tone of thine.

No babe could repose on a fond Mother's breast
  More calmly confiding than I do on thine;
I fly to thy arms, as a bird to its nest,
  For shelter and safety, dear Husband of mine!

Aye, "Mine, and mine only!" Oh, joy passing words!
  To carol this song in my innermost heart;
" While thine, and thine only ! " the vibrating chords
  Shall echo till sense, life, and feeling depart.

ISAB. B.

THE DEAD CHIEF.*

(HAVELOCK.)

PILLOWED on his Indian bed,
   England's gallant hero lies—
Sheathed his good sword, bowed his head,
   Passed his soul into the skies;
 Widows weep around his grave,
   Orphans' tears fall thick and fast—
Ever thus should sleep the brave,
   When the war of life is past!

Time will tell the deeds he wrought
   With his trusty, stainless blade—
How he suffered, how he fought
   'Ere he in the earth was laid;

---

* Music by R. F. LÖWELL; published by J. H. JEWELL, Gt. Russell St., W.C.

Time will brand the Nena's guilt,
　　Time will gild our Havelock's fame—
Who the blood of woman spilt,
　　Who avenged that deed of shame.

Think we well of him, and hold
　　Bravely to the life he spent—
Write his name in words of gold
　　On the World's vast monument;
Soldier-hero! Christian-man!
　　Self-enobled; let him rest,
Kinglier in the warrior van
　　Than with stars upon his breast!

　　　　　　　　　　　　G. L. B.

MIDNIGHT BY THE SEA.

———

ALONE, by night, I take my way
  Where wild waves dash upon the shore,
And listen to the plaintive lay
  Sung by Old Ocean evermore,
In memory of those who sleep
Down in the bosom of the Deep.

The midnight stars, with silent tread,
  The azure heavens march along,
To strains of music overhead
  Returning a triumphant song
Of morn to come—of day to be
Ere long throughout eternity.

O, glorious stars! O, mighty Deep!
　　Who sing the Living and the Dead,
Let grief no more our eyelids steep
　　In tears unprofitably shed—
For every riven link of love
A star in glory shines above!

　　　　　　　　　　　　　G. L. B.

DECEIVED!

On the shore of a tranquil lake
 A maiden reclined and dreamed
Of the hearts she would win and break
 While that summer sunlight beamed;
She mused o'er her victories past,
 Of her captives yet to be;
And the spells she would round them cast
 To bring them down to her knee.

On the shore of a troubled lake
 A maiden wandered alone,
'Mong the hearts she had vowed to break
 She had not counted her own;
But a brighter eye than her own,
 A tongue as false and as fair
Won her soul with a look and a tone,
 Then left her to love and despair.

       Isab. B.

MAKE WAY!

.

———

AN ANTHEM FOR THE PEOPLE.

.   ———

" Pomp and Pride, Wealth and Birth,
These have had their reign on earth,
Each has had its little day,
Each in turn must pass away."

Thus, as Life's watch-tower I climb,
'Twixt Eternity and Time,
Looking out into the night
For a glimpse of morning light,
Spirit-voices floating near
Prophecy unto mine ear—
        Solemn voices,
        Preacher voices,

From the pulpit of the age
  Minist'ring the truths of old,
Written in the sacred page
  With a pen of fire and gold.
    Soft and low
    They come and go,
While far down the anxious crowd,
Weary watchers cry aloud :—
  "Watchman ! tell us of the night ?
  Tell us of the morning light?
  Worn and weary, when will Day
  Roll along the people's way ? "

Up the morn, like breath of flowers,
Gently steal the new-born hours,
Back night's spectral shadows fly
Gloomily, despondingly—
Hark ! the tramp of many feet—
Hark ! the voices of the street—
    Rugged voices,
    Earnest voices
Rising now and borne along
In the majesty of song :—

"Night is gone, Day comes on ;
    Breaks the morning clear and strong—
Stand aside, Pomp and Pride,
    Let the People move along !"

Spirits of the past called back
From Death's silent dusty track—
Mighty spirits, patriots, sages,
Beacon lights through endless ages—
Come with faces lank and pale
Telling each its own dread tale
Of injustice meekly borne,
Honest service met by scorn—
    Ghastly faces,
    Ah, me ! faces
That appal the eyes of men,
Jabbering "Amen !" "Amen !"
To the burden of the throng,
Swelling deep, and loud, and strong :—
    "Night is gone, Day comes on,
        Breaks the morning clear and strong—
    Stand aside, Wealth and Pride,
        Let the People move along !"

" Why should Genius, why should Worth—
God's nobilities on earth,—
Why should Labour, God's right hand,
Be accursed in the land ?"
Cries the Spirit of the hour,
Sentinel in Life's watch-tower—
        Answer echo,
        " Wherefore ?" echo,
And the low'ring heavens reply
In thunders rolling through the sky :—
    " Night is gone, Day comes on,
      Breaks the morning clear and strong—
    Stand aside, Birth and Pride,
      Let the People move along !"

Lowly tillers of the soil,
Free from battle, blood, or spoil ;
Craftsmen whose inventive skill
Moulds the elements at will ;
Lion-hearts that wield the Pen
To shape the destinies of men—
        Scourge of sinners,
        Conflict winners,

Ye have given the honest lie
To class distinctions, hence the cry :—
    " Night is gone, Day comes on,
        Breaks the morning clear and strong—
    Stand aside, Power and Pride,
        Let the people move along !"

Sing the dawning of the morn
When the world is newly born !
Sing the people's jubilee,
Thankfully, exultingly !
Sing the fall of huge pretence !
Sing the commonwealth of sense !
Sing the reign of Christ below !
Sing Appolyon's overthrow !
        Plodding mortal,
        Fortune's portal
Opens wide to thee and thine,
Followers in a glorious line !
        At the last
        Sweepeth past

The mighty mandate of High Heaven
In strains of men and angels given;
At last old prejudices die
And everywhere the nations cry:—
 " Night is gone, Day comes on,
  Breaks the morning clear and strong—
 Stand aside, Pomp and Pride,
  Let the People move along!"

G. L. B.

DREAMS OF AN ENTHUSIAST.

" Gleamings of poetry—if I may give
That name of beauty, passion, and of grace,
To the wild thoughts that in a starlit hour,
In a pale twilight, or a rosebud morn,
Glance o'er my spirit—thoughts that are like light,
Or love, or hope, in their effects."

LANDON.

I HAVE been long a Dreamer, and have lived
'Mid an ideal world of untamed thoughts,
That gushed with wild exuberance, and laid
My spirit in a trance of rich delight,
Delicious, rapturous; and yet—ah, me!—
Lacking the words to pour their magic forth
Clad in a fitting garb ;—meagre and scant
The wordy wardrobe under my control.
In vain, in vain, bright fancies woo my pen,
Flitting athwart my visionary brain
As lights electric 'cross an arctic sky ;
Fitful and fleeting, vainly do they gleam
Ineffably effulgent o'er my mind,

Shedding their halo over all within.

If language be denied.   My spirit yearns

And pants for freedom from its bondage ;—thoughts

And feelings, far too rapt for utterance,

O'erflow the hidden fountains of my soul,

Swelling the tide of my ideas.   Still,

Though thought pours onward in a mighty flood,

A vast, illimitable stream, its course

Is desultory, undefined, and needs

A channel more restrained, whose marge, besprent

With fairest flowers of eloquence, and draped

With rich expression's graceful foliage,

Should mete the brimming stream of thought, and guide

It onward in a path of song.

                My dreams,

In rosy childhood's hours, were all bedight

With gorgeous palaces and glistening gems,

So costly that a single one had been

The ample purchase of a kingdom.   Elves

And fairies were around me, and I roved

'Mid Fancy's mad creations,—Fairy-land

Was my tranced spirit's home.   I looked abroad

Through a prismatic glass of magic mould,
That tinted all things with its vivid hues.
I pored in a delighted ecstasy
Over Silesia's legendary lore,
Until each castle and each forest shade
Seemed filled with spirit-shapes; and every breeze
That wantoned lightly by, and kissed my cheek,
Was as a wood-nymph's blossom-scented breath.
The bubbling well from mossy covert burst,
And laved my lingering feet, as I beheld
Th' ideal dweller in this liquid shrine;—
Each woodland rill, each tree-o'er-shadowed stream,
To me was vocal with a Naiad's song
Of invitation to her crystal haunt.
The Demon of the Hartz was aye to me
An unresisting slave : his pine-tree staff
Shivered the rocky gates that hid from sight
The subterraneous caverns of his realm,
And at my beck unearthed the dwarfy gnomes
Who clustered round, like swarms of unhived bees.

Such were my dreams by day ; and when the night
Came, heralded by Hesperus, my head,

Play-weary, courted sleep in its retreat,
And won the prize of rest; then,—if the day
Were bright with joyous images,—did night
Blaze with superb magnificence, that far
Outshone my waking fancies. Terrible,
Yet splendid, in their majesty sublime,
Stood the stern Genii of famed Araby,
Trampling on jewels radiant with light,
As 'twere on worthless dust, and scattering gold
Upon their favourites with lavish hands.
And then the Peri; oh! most beautiful
Her love-expressing countenance, that shone
As with the rays of her lost paradise,
Yet seemed most mournful in its loveliness,
As though regret yet lingered there, and made
Pensive her floating eye. Her half-closed wing
Gleamed like the rainbow's many-coloured arch
Expanding into gorgeousness; her lips
Knew only how to bless. And I awoke
To the realities of day, but to regret
The vanished visions of the sleepy night.

Then came, with time, the stores of classic Greece :
Olympus was my fancy's resting place,

Where I confronted eagle-mounted Jove,
And from the cup of youthful Ganymede
Tasted the luscious nectar. Juno, too,
In stately dignity appeared, and sought
For universal homage.   Then came one
Perfect in every charm of loveliness :—
A dimpled form, symmetrically just
In all its wavy outlines ; gracefulness
In every look and gesture, and a skin
Clear and transparent, delicately tinged
The pinky hue of sunrise upon snow ;
Her only robe a mantle of rich curls,
Glittering like interwoven rays, obtained
From Sol, by force or stratagem, when he
Erewhile his nightly couch in ocean prest,—
Ere Venus, queen of love and beauty, rose
To gladden eyes immortal.   I, gazing,
Mused on her ill-assorted union
With Vulcan, the deformed.

                Then Mercury,
On ever-restless wings, came flitting past,—
The courier of the gods. My " willing feet "
Strayed to Thessalian Tempé—lingered by

The Muses' sacred fount, and visited
Their temple on Parnassus.   Orpheus then
My dreaming ear with sounds Elysian tranced,
And charmed my listening soul with music's spell.
When twilight's deepening shades veiled the dim woods,
Oft have I loitered in some lone retreat,
And, peering through long vistas of tall trees,
With apt Imagination's ready aid,
Peopled the woods with Dryads, Satyrs, Fauns,
Who danced in hilarous glee to the wild strains
Of Pan's untutored reed, or singly sought
To twine the pliant branches of young trees
Into fantastic knots.   And Zephyrus,
Wooing the lovely Flora with soft sighs,
Came by me, laden with the fragrancy
He sipped from her sweet lips.

                              The sea's clear waves,
Clashing like cymbals, voiced the Tritons' song,
And I have gazed into its azure depths
With feelings undefinable.   Transports
Of strange wild character have thrilled my frame,

And impulses, nigh irresistible,
Have tempted me to plunge beneath the wave,
And dive to Neptune's coral-pillared halls,
In search of Ocean's mysteries.   The shells
Left on the shore by the receding tide,—
Nereid coracles, deserted by
The tiny feet that prest them ; whence adieus
Seemed murmured plainingly, in low soft tones,
To their false fairy pilots ; and the light
Phosphoric of the element that zones
Our terraqueous globe, gleams upward cast,
From lamps illumining sea's amber caves,
As for a spirit festival.

                        Then, dreams
Were mine of that arch-hypocrite, young Love,—
Of all my phantasies the most untrue.
I pictured him a pure bright deity,
And worshipped at his shrine at morn and eve,
At midnight's stilly hour, and day's hot noon.
Love seemed the life of life,—th' essential part
Of animate existence ; every thought

And feeling merged into that single one,

Till love seemed wedded unto happiness.

Love blinds his visionary votaries,

And blissful they who never lift the veil,

Or tear the fillet from the mental eye.

Alas! the band was rent aside from mine,

And I was taught, too soon, that I had dreamed

As I could dream no more!

      But now, again,

My visionary soul is pilgrim led

Unto the land of everlasting rest,

And, as in childhood, my bright thoughts are blest

With radiant shapes, and daylight never dim.

But all too exquisite for pen to paint,

The inexpressible effulgence shed

Over the dreamy future, by the wings

Of the angelic sentinels who guard

The dazzling gates of Paradise, and sound,

With golden trumpets, an awakening blast

To the long slumbering dreamer.

         Isab. B

OUT IN THE WORLD.

———

Out in the World I can but feel
   The stings of which the world is full,
A thousand cares around me steal,
   The streets are cold, the skies are dull—
Friends pass me by who oft have sat
   And quaffed the best my board could show ;
Down o'er my brow I pull my hat
   And inly ponder as I go :
But when I reach my own hearth-stone,
   And sit amidst my girls and boys,
I taste of raptures few have known,
   And feel that life is crowned with joys.

Out in the World I meet with men
On 'Change or in the merchant throng,
Who plot and scheme, and use the pen
For objects fraudulent and wrong:
Their scrip is false, their bills are bad,
Their pomp and state a huge pretence—
The hat comes down, and I grow sad
At human nature's impotence:
But when I seek my own hearth-stone,
And sit amidst my girls and boys,
I taste of raptures few have known,
And feel that life is crowned with joys.

Out in the world nought else is seen
But Fashion's votaries flaunting by,
And Pride decked out in crinoline
To give humanity the lie;
Conceit runs riot, purse runs out,
Ruin and misery warfare wage;
The hat comes down—I turn about
And mourn the follies of the age.

But when I seek my own hearth-stone
  And sit amidst my girls and boys,
I taste of raptures few have known,
  And feel that life is crowned with joys.

Out in the world the smoothest face
  (Though falsehood lurk beneath the skin)
Is foremost in the golden race,—
  Blunt honesty may seldom win;
Lands, houses, deeds, usurp the power
  Affection in the heart should hold;
Down comes the hat, O cursed hour!
  And doubly cursed greed of gold!
But when I reach my own hearth-stone,
  And sit amidst my girls and boys,
I taste of raptures few have known,
  And feel that life is crowned with joys.

                              G. L. B.

THE ABSENT ONE.

THE one I love she is not here—
    She is not here, but far away
And I am drooping, like the flowers,
    That bend their heads at close of day ;
When shall I hear again the tones
    That first disturbed my dream of peace ?
When fold her fondly in my arms,
    And bid this hidden tumult cease ?

Alas ! that those who are akin
    In all that lends a charm to life,
Should be estranged e'en for an hour
    By time or chance—by word or strife ;
But so it is, the fairest scene
    Basks not for ever in the sun,
But fades into the silent night
    When day its golden course has run.

G. L. B.

A HOME SONG FOR HOME BIRDS.*

(TO MY HUSBAND.)

Wearily, drearily linger the hours
    Parted from thee love, parted from thee;
Life seems a wilderness barren of flowers
    Absent from thee love, absent from thee;
"Home!" is the cry of my desolate heart,
Home! for home only can be where thou art!

Merrily, cheerily frolic the hours
    Passed in thy presence love, lit by thine eye;
Love blunts the thorns of life's rose-covered bowers
    When thou art nigh love, when thou art nigh:
"Home!" is the cry of my innermost heart,
Home! for 'tis home, love, wherever thou art!

ISAB. B.

* Music by W. T. BELCHER.

LABOUR'S FESTIVAL!

———

An Ode, written for the West London Industrial Exhibition, and delivered by Mr. Edmund Phelps, May 1st, 1865.

———

PART FIRST.

MAY the Enchantress! hitherward hies
    Crowned with her hawthorn wreath—
With gleams of light in her sunny eyes
    And perfume on her breath ;
She comes with the pleasant song of birds,
    The tinkle of woodland rills,
And the distant lowing of scattered herds
    . 'Mongst the daisied meads and hills ;
Beautiful May ! we welcome her here,
The Queen of the Spring-tide! the Bride of the Year !

PART SECOND.

We welcome the May, for she brings in her train
Far more than the promise of blossom or grain—
Far more than the tinkle of brooklet and rill ;
She brings us the products of Labour and Skill !

Not from the factory crowded with hands—
Not from the workshop, where men toil in bands—
Not from the foundry, the mart, or the quay,
Brings she these products—the Beautiful May !

Offshoots of fancy, the solace of years—
Creatures of discipline, baptised in tears—
Nurslings of genius neglected in youth—
Ministers all, of Life, Beauty, and Truth !

Humble the hands which these treasures have wrought ;
Humble the homesteads from which they were brought ;
But fashioned 'mid hardships that make work sublime,
They are bright, precious gems in the Casket of Time !

PART THIRD.

Men of the rough and horny hand!
　　Men of the stern and sweat-dewed brow!
True heroes on the field of Life,
　　The world beholds your triumphs now;
Proud, of a truth, may be the land
　　That's privileged to see ye strive;
Sedition cannot lift its head
　　Within the honey-storing hive.

Ye toil for bread, to eat and live,
　　But in that toil of hand and brain
The will of Providence is sown
　　To ripen into golden grain;
With humble means, by slow degrees,
　　From strength to strength ye higher rise—
Like trees whose roots are in the earth,
　　Whose branches soar unto the skies.

To-day, ye write with golden pen
　　Upon the world's historic page,
The progress made by Working Men
　　From serfdom's dawn to freedom's age:

G

How, free in person, home, and thought,
   Ye use the freedom wisely given,
For which your fathers toiled and fought—
   For which yourselves at times have striven

How artisans, in leisure free,
   Have turned to arts not all their own,
And stamped each mind's identity
   On canvas, metal, wood, or stone;
Have proved their right to take a place
   As thinking workers on the soil—
As leaders in the upward race,
   Ennobled not by birth—but Toil.

CHORUS.

Peace crown this day—this thrice-blessed, happy day!
The First of May—the Workman's Holiday!
When flowers of Spring and flowers of Toil unite
To fill our souls with wonder and delight.
Peace crown this day! and everlasting love
Descend upon us from the realms above!

                               G. L. B.

A BEGGAR'S PETITION.

FOR MY ALBUM

Spirits of Pencil and of Pen,
  Twin genii of Fame,
Pause in your swift career awhile,
  And list my earnest claim ;
Touch with your magic wands my book
  'Till every leaf and page
Glows with the tints or lines of thought
  Of Painter, Poet, Sage.

Give me to feel that here has throbbed
  The living pulse of mind—
That hands instinct with human life
  My Album wreath have twined—

That no cold type-interpreter
   Here comes our souls between,
But I may commune with the great—
   Be where the great have been.

Cast then within my treasury
   Your gems and flowers of thought,
Gifts, precious from their rarity,
   Priceless, because unbought;
And though my thanks may be unheard
   They will be deep and true;
So now—my hopes and claims preferred,
   I leave the rest to you.

ISAB. B.

SABBATH ASPIRATIONS.

———

ARK of the soul!—God's gift —sweet Sabbath morn,
  Riding for ever 'mid the world's unrest,
While peace and joy—twin ministers, new-born—
  Set up their golden altar in the breast;
What sound can equal the persuasive chime
  Of thy sweet bells, soft floating on the air?
Calling poor mortals, by the voice of time,
  To bow their spirits in the house of prayer.

Who bows not meekly at the Throne of Grace,
  Pleading the mortal weaknesses of man,
Turneth from world-embracing love his face,
  And, leagued with devils, fights in Falsehood's van;

The stream of mercy, issuing from the Throne,
   To him no hope, no comfort sweet can bring;
He walks the earth, in darkness and alone,
   A puny, grovelling, leprous, soulless thing.

But, O, for him who treads down human pride,
   And rises pure in thought to Heaven's gate;
Who roams in spirit through its mansions wide,
   Where angel hosts on Deity await;
He has the world's broad sunshine on his brow—
   He has another sunshine in his heart —
And, whether taken from the court or plough,
   Is crowned by God when summoned to depart!

Two paths there are for mortal man to tread:
   One leads to glory—one to grief and shame.
Who takes the former proudly bears his head—
   A heavenly grandeur shapes his every aim;
He rides upon the storm-cloud in repose,
   Fearless of ill.   Not so the world's unblest:
They are the sport of every wind that blows —
   Of demon passions raging in the breast.

Lead us, great God! by Thy green pastures fair,
   Where Thy sun shines, and Thy pure waters flow;
Lead us from worldly wrong, and greed, and care,
   Into that life whence Christian graces grow;
Lead us to Thy great worship, void of art,
   Of pompous pageant and ascetic creed;
Who covet forms can know Thee but in part—
   Who turn to Thee, alone, are Thine indeed.

Who bow to Thee in secret—lift the soul
   In solemn silence to Thy mercy-seat—
Through their poor veins what rapt emotions roll!
   What aspirations course with flying feet!
Earth fades, as 'twere a meteor's falling ray;
   A solemn anthem swell breaks on the ear;
The pall of night rolls up in endless day,
   And Thou, the dread Omnipotent, art near!

Fain would we ever 'neath Thy wing repose,
   Sheltered, protected—Thou, great God! our friend.
Strengthen our souls to triumph o'er all foes,
   Aid us to fight Life's battle to the end;

E'en as brave soldiers, summoned to the field,
    Flash their good swords, till, stretched upon the sod,
Into Thy hands our spirits would we yield,
    Struck down whilst fighting in Thy cause, O God!

G. L. B.

THE LEAF AND THE SOUL.

———

" How like am I to thee, old leaf !
   We'll drop together down ;
How like art thou to me, old leaf !
   We'll drop together down.
I'm grey, and thou art brown, old leaf !
We'll drop together down, old leaf !
   We'll drop together down.

" Drop, drop into the grave, old leaf !
   Drop, drop into the grave ;
Thy acorn's grown, thy acorn's sown,
   Drop, drop into the grave."

                 —EBENEZER ELLIOTT.

———

THOU wilt drop into the grave, old leaf !
   And, blending with the soil,
Resign existence, fluttering, brief,
   Death's undisputed spoil.
The Spring may come, with bud and bloom —
Spring may not call thee from the tomb.

Thou wilt drop into the grave, old leaf,
    Earth will demand its own,
And the oak that wears thee, without grief,
    Return earth's summer loan ;
Then bid the light and sun adieu,
No future may thy life renew.

Thou wilt drop into the grave, old man,
    And mingle with the mould ;
Thou mayst linger yet a few years' span,—
    Soon will their date be told ;
And thy God-fashioned form of clay
Will moulder silently away.

If the perishable part must sink
    Into the silent grave,
And time dissever Life's frail link,—
    Thou hast a soul to save :
Thou art *not* like the fragile leaf,—
Death ushers thee to joy or grief.

                    Isab. B.

TO MY WIFE.

On the Anniversary of her Birthday, March 25th, 1865.

I LOVED you when I saw you first
   With all the love my heart could hold,
And 'twas not little since it lasts
   When we're mid-aged and growing old;
A lighter step was yours that time,
   A sunnier gleam played on your brow,
But mirrored in dear memory
   What you were then, I see you now.

Some storms have broken o'er our path,
   Some serpents crawled along our way,
And we have seen the little ones
   We hoped to rear, alas! decay:

Still, by God's providence preserved,
    Some precious joys around us cling,
And blest with you and our three bairns
    I feel as happy as a king.

Would I were worthier of one
    Whose daily course has gone to prove
How gifts and goodness may unite
    In all a Wife's and Mother's love ;
But take me, Dearest, humanly,
    With all my faults, unworthy thee,
And love me, not for what I am,
    But what in heart I wish to be.

G. L. B.

MY HOME IS ON THE MOUNTAIN STEEP.*

My home is on the mountain steep,
Far away—far away,
Where the playful chamois leap,
All the day—all the day.
Oft in sunny dreams of joy,
Glad and eager as a boy,
Do I climb each Alpine height,
Led away in Fancy's flight
To the well-known mountain steep,
Far away—far away,
Where the playful chamois leap,
All the day—all the day.

* Music by W. T. BELCHER. Published by J. II. JEWELL & Co.

For years I've roamed the stranger's shore,
    Young and free—young and free,
Yet my spirit pines the more,
    Home to see—home to see.
Though each scene is fair and bright,
Turns my heart in fond delight
To the old romantic spot
Where still stands my father's cot,
    High upon the mountain steep,
      Far away—far away,
    Where the playful chamois leap,
      All the day—all the day.

                        G. L. B.

THE SEEN AND UNSEEN.

THERE are spots in ocean's bed
    No plummet line may sound,
There are sands no foot may tread ;
And bright stars overhead
    No telescope hath found.

So in the human soul
    Are depths no eye may reach,
Whose tide may surge and roll,
Strong passions 'neath control—
    Emotions without speech !

Shut in the heart's deep core,
    Lie action's secret springs,
Dread and solemn evermore,
As the unknown Arctic shore,
    Or Future's unseen wings.

We may live without disguise,
    May lay the pure heart bare,
But never to lip may rise,
From that temple's mysteries,
    All that lies throbbing there.

If the heart of Nature hold
    Its secrets close and deep,
So the human breast may fold
A world of thought, untold
    In still and voiceless sleep

And but He who veiled the shrine
    Of individual thought,
Ere may lift that veil divine,
See what weapons gleam and shine
    As life's long fight is fought.

                         ISAB. B.

SONGS OF THE SEASONS.*

SPRING.

SWEET Spring is coming,
   Coming through the dell,
Zephyrs are humming
   Winter's long farewell;
Primroses springing
   Deck the verdant lea,
Wild birds are singing
   On the hawthorn tree;
In mid-heaven shining,
   Joy the sun doth bring,
All life combining
   Ushers in the Spring.

* The whole of these songs are arranged as four part-songs by W. T.
BELCHER; published by J. H. JEWELL, Great Russell Street.

H

Sweet Spring is coming,
    Coming o'er the wild,
Sweet, and blithe, and bonnie
    As a fairy child.

Sweet Spring is coming,
    Coming o'er the hill,
Where the hare-bell dances
    To the murmuring rill ;
Kingcups bright and golden
    Peep a-down the vale,
Violets unfolden
    Scent the passing gale ;
Merrily the Cuckoo
    In the woods is heard,
Singing " Cuckoo, Cuckoo "—
    Bless the wandering bird !
Sweet Spring is coming,
    Coming o'er the wild,
Sweet, and blithe, and bonnie
    As a fairy child.

SUMMER.

CROWNED with blushing roses bright,
　　Wreathed with tender lilies pale,
Summer wings her joyous flight
　　On the balmy breathing gale;
　　　　Wee ones bless her,
　　　　Winds caress her,
　　Young buds nestle at her feet.
　　　　Love rejoices,
　　　　All earth's voices
　　Sing her praise in accents sweet.

Crowned with blushing roses bright,
　　Wreathed with tender lilies pale,
Summer wings her joyous flight
　　On the balmy breathing gale.

Where the early wakened bee
　　Toileth for his honied cells—
Where the fairies half in glee
　　Hide amongst the heather bells,
　　　　Summer lingers
　　　　With light fingers
　　　　　　H 2

Bathing buds in morning light,
Leaf and blossom
On her bosom
Fondly folding through the night.

Crowned with blushing roses bright,
Wreathed with tender lilies pale,
Summer wings her joyous flight
On the balmy breathing gale.

———

AUTUMN.

The ripe fruits mellow in the sun,
The laden boughs are hanging down,
The summer flowers to seed have run,
The forest leaves are ting'd with brown,
The poppy gems the yellow corn,
The leveret scents the new-mown hay,
And rising with the early morn
The merry reaper takes his way—

Full and round the harvest moon,
Sweet and clear the harvest tune,
Light and mirth o'er all the land
Greet the merry harvest band.

The truant bird is on the wing,
  The sportsman out upon the moor,
And laughing children dance and sing
  At sunset round the cottage door;
For Spring may clothe the naked ground,
  And Summer give the roses birth—
But Autumn comes with plenty crown'd,
  And scatters blessings o'er the earth.

        Full and round the harvest moon,
        Sweet and clear the harvest tune,
        Light and mirth o'er all the land,
        Greet the merry harvest band.

————

WINTER.

GIVE me the lusty Winter time
  When storm and cloud sweep by,
And winds ring out their midnight chime
  In the belfry of the sky;
        Though burly
        And surly,

And ominous and drear—
It sets the old hearth blazing,
And brings the best o' cheer !

Let snowflakes tuft the frozen ground,
　Or cap the distant hill,
And stream and torrent both be bound
　By Winter's iron will ;
　　　Though freezing
　　　And teasing
To those whom he comes near—
He kindles warmth in many a heart,
And brings the best o' cheer !

If days are short, the nights are long,
　Why then need we complain,
Since night brings round the merry song
　And merrier refrain—
　　　All joining,
　　　Combining
To dry the passing tear ?
Ah ! Winter is a jovial time,
And brings the best 'o cheer !

Then give me jovial Winter, boys,
   And true hearts all around
To share the deep if transient joys
   That in its reign are found!
      Friends meeting,
      Hearts beating
In fellowship sincere :
O, Winter is a jovial time,
And brings the best o' cheer!

G. L. B.

THE NEGLECTED WIFE.

Our radiant Queen of Night,—the crescent moon,
Closely companioned by a host of stars
That troop around her like a body guard,
Has reached her climax in the firmament;
And, lighting up the heavy dew that drips
From the closed petals of each sleeping flower,
Makes every bough a mimic chandelier
Festooned with diamonds.   'Tis such a night
As makes a lovely scene still lovelier,
And even flings a kind of quiet charm
Over the city's clustering roofs,—the homes
Of those whom daylight calls to congregate
Within its now deserted streets and squares ;—
Where, wrapt in slumb'rous quietude, the sons
Of Traffic, Mammon's votaries, the slaves

Who bend obsequiously to Fashion,
The poor—the rich, the strong and feeble now
To Nature's nightly dictates yield.   Somnus
And Morpheus hold high festival, and bind
Their passive captives in a deathlike trance,
Reigning o'er prostrate strength and dormant mind.

   Yet *one* there is who bows not 'neath their sway,—
By whom the loveliness of earth and sky
Is viewed with apathy, or unobserved.
Her husband is a truant from his home,—
Haply engaged in noisy revelry,
And she, with uncomplaining, patient love,
Anxiously waits his long-delayed return.
Yet once—and that so short a time agone,
It seems but yesterday—her slightest word, —
A half-breathed wish, had brought him to her side ;
And he would linger there as if entranced,
Hanging upon each syllable she breathed,
As life or death depended on her word.
And then, with voice all gently tuned to love,
He vowed—and she, alas ! weak girl, believed !—

To love her until death ; still to be true
Though all beside were false,—to be her shield
'Gainst life's vicissitudes,—to guard her form
From blighting care, or undermining grief;
To be through life a fond and steadfast friend,
On whom she might, with confidence, rely
For comfort in affliction,—whose deep love
Would echo back her own, and in whose heart
Her image lay enshrined, as his in hers.
And she had listened to his pleading tones
Until her love became imperative,
And she forgot that promises are frail,
And so became his bride.

                              And how kept he
Those promises?   Ask the neglected Wife!
Look on her fading cheeks ;—the hectic flush
That flits across their snow, like memory
Of former blushes now revisiting
The ruins of their home,—the tears that steal
Silently down that Parian cheek, and hang
Like rain-drops on a lily ; these reveal

How well the Husband kept the Lover's vow.

The night wears on apace, she trims her lamp,—

Its light was burning dimly, like her hopes;

She takes a book, and strives to fix her eye

And mind upon the tale,—how vain a task !

In a strange chaos blent, the letters seem

To dance confusedly o'er the unread page,

And mock her aching sight. She *cannot* read,—

Her thoughts *will* wander forth. At every sound

She starts, as if in hope; a step is heard

Approaching,—breathlessly she listens till

The footstep passes by ; and then she sighs,

Haply in sympathy for those who mourn

That absentee from home. And then she counts

The sluggish footfalls of the drowsy hours,

As the dull pendulum, with lazy swing,

Beats time to each slow step. How heavily

Time hangs upon the hands of those who wait

With anxious expectations, unfulfilled,

Which time must gratify ! She pauses oft,

And bends her head as in the attitude

Of an attentive listener, in hope

To catch the earliest sound that heralds

His approach.   She may resume the volume
Her eye is toiling o'er,—it is not he.
Poor watcher! thy lot indeed is sadness,
Doomed as thou art to pass life's glowing noon
In solitary vigils like to this,
Which, not the first, will scarcely be the last.
But hark! another footstep comes,—"'Tis he!"
She flies to meet him, and the ready smile
Welcomes the truant home.   Too glad to chide,
She utters no reproach,—upbraids him not
For his repeated absence, his neglect;
She only feels that he is now at home,
Within her circling arms,—that her lone watch
Is ended for the night; and the rebuke
Dies on her trembling lips, that breathe but joy
For his long-sought return!

                            Oh, ye who mock
At woman's quenchless love, ask your cold hearts
If ye could watch thus patiently for hours,
Weary and dull, debarred of needful rest,
With no companion save your own sad thoughts,—

Few gleams of hope to bear your spirits up,
And retrospections that but chill the more
From contrast with the present ; and then own
That man, unstable man, possesses not
This long-enduring love, this steady faith,
Patient forbearance, self-forgetfulness,
This deep devotion of the heart to love,
Which thus enables woman to endure
Trials that man, with all his vaunted strength,
Would shrink from in dismay.   He *would not* sit
In solitary loneliness, to muse
O'er an ungrateful wife, then cheerfully
Woo back the rover to his heart and home
With smiles of happiness !   No, he would seek
Redress for wrong.   *This* woman *cannot* do :
Weak woman still must bear, contentedly,
The countless wrongs man heaps upon her head
With uncomplaining fortitude.   Murmurs
From woman's lips are treason in his sight.—
" She is the weaker vessel," man asserts,
Yet loads her straining heart as though it were
But to refute his doctrine ; for she proves
In trial's hour the *stronger !*

ISAB. B

CALCRAFT'S CARNIVAL.

A PROTEST AGAINST CAPITAL PUNISHMENT.

A SEA of heads below,
  Of congregated faces,
Huddled and packed to show
  How limited the space is ;
Ten thousand look like one,
  Fathers, children, and mothers—
Ten thousand are as one,
  Erring sisters and brothers.   .

A glare of upturned eyes,
  Basilisks wildly staring ;
Lips unparted by sighs,
  But oaths and curses sharing ;

Blasphemy, jest, and song,
   Bandied in wild disorder—
Stories of culprits hung,
   Greenacre, Rush, and Corder.

O, what a harvest time
   For dens and public-houses !
A festival of crime
   When each vile wretch carouses !
O, what a dainty day
   For letting window places
Where in the sun's bright ray
   Now bask those human faces !

Thieves are plying their trade,
   The lost—abandoned, drinking ;
Criminals being made,
   No sense of pain or shrinking ;
Voices rending the air,
   Volley succeeding volley,
From hearts consumed by care
   Yet striving to be "jolly."

O, what a raging hell
　Lighteth those upturned features !
O, what an evil spell
　Curseth those mingling creatures !
Fiercer the rabble shout,
　As the victim seems to falter.
Alas !—the ill poured out
　On that mass, like poisoned water.

There—on the scaffold drear,
　Before death's open portal,
Trembling with shame and fear,
　Bends the accursed mortal :
With a despairing look,
　" Mercy, O Christ ! " he shrieketh—
Closed is the chaplain's book,
　That of ONE ATONEMENT speaketh.

A shrill moan of despair
　As the signal dread is given—
And he dangleth in the air,
　Midway 'twixt earth and heaven ;

Like a dog that hath no soul,
 With writhed and blackening features
Thrust down to death's dread goal,
 By erring human creatures.

Homeward the masses trail
 To haunts of destitution,
Where children stunted, pale,
 Feed, gloat upon pollution ;
Where "gin," and dirt, and crime,
 And natures coarse and callous
Are breeding in human slime
 Work for the hulks and gallows.

Thus murder is reproved !
 Of course, the world's condition
Is very much improved
 By such an exhibition !
Alas! alas ! the day !
 Of that vast throng, so "jolly,"
Not *one* but goes away
 More hardened in his folly !

       G. L. B.

I

THE DISH WITH A COVER.

———

(WHAT I SAW, AND WHAT I THOUGHT.)

———

I SING a song of an earthenware dish,
But whether it held or fowl or fish,
Or something not so daintyish,
    Was a secret hid by the cover.

'Twas held by a hand, with a glove of kid,
Was that earthenware dish with the friendly lid,
But what that dish or that drapery hid,
    Could not be seen through the cover.

A footman opened the mansion gate
To let out the lady, who carried in state
That *something* to put on a cottager's plate,
    Which was hid by the friendly cover.

By the longest path, in the open day,
That lady and dish went their public way :
But was it charity or display
    Brought round that dish with the cover ?

That lady-like hand must needs be strong,
Since she carried the dish so far and long,
That the something meant for spoon or prong
    Went cold underneath the cover.

If the hearts that beat in a cottage home
Have pulses like those 'neath a lordly dome,
Pain, as well as a dinner, might come
    On that dish beneath the cover.

Kindness of heart might prompt the deed,
To help the sick or the poor in their need,
But one article in our Christian creed
    Says—" Do thine alms under cover!"

The mantle wide to cover our sin,
Is not to flaunt o'er the highways in,
But to wear unseen by kith or kin
    When we carry a dish with a cover.

That lady's gift might be great or small,
But coming in state, as it did, from the Hall,
It seemed to come with a trumpet call
    For the passers to gaze at the cover.

But here let us spread the mantle wide,
And hope that the dish contained inside
A dinner without a spice of pride
    To poison it under the cover.

And be it by each and all confest,
There are secret motives in every breast,
Acts do not always the heart attest—
    Each carries a dish with a cover.

                         ISAB. B.

O, BARD OF GENTLE AVON! *

Written for the Shakespeare Tercentenary Celebration, and sung by Madame Parepa, April 23rd, 1864.

Of all the names that proudly live
    Enshrined in song or story,
And to the world's great annals give
    A golden gleam of glory,
One name there is, one mighty name,
    With rev'rent love we cherish,
The foremost in the scroll of Fame,
    The last through time to perish.
        O, Bard of gentle Avon!
        Sweet Bard of gentle Avon!
        From age to age in thine own page,
        Thy fame lives, Bard of Avon!

* Music by G. A. MACFARREN; published by the London Music Publishing Company.

Oft nature wills the great shall spring
From homesteads men call lowly;
A neatherd's roof has held a King
Who made its hearthstone holy:
So Shakspeare, England's Minstrel King,
Went out from peasant's portal,
To sit on Fancy's Throne, and sing
Songs that should be immortal.
O, Bard of gentle Avon!
Sweet Bard of gentle Avon!
From age to age in thine own page,
Thy fame lives, Bard of Avon!

Of Troy the Bard of Chios sang,
Love-fashioned Petrarch's measure,
Anacreon's lyre alternate rang
Inspired by wine and pleasure:
But he, who Heaven's warrant held
To sing of all creation,
The universal soul compelled
To give him inspiration.

O, Bard of gentle Avon !
Sweet Bard of gentle Avon !
From age to age, in thine own page,
Thy fame lives, Bard of Avon !

Then twine the Amaranth and Bay,
　And let the wide world know it :
We crown with hallowed hands to-day
　Our land's Immortal Poet.
If death and darkness hold his dust,
　His spirit lingers near us,
Still faithful to its ancient trust,
　To counsel, guide, and cheer us.
　　　O, Bard of gentle Avon !
　　　Sweet Bard of gentle Avon !
　　　From age to age, in thine own page,
　　　Thy fame lives, Bard of Avon !

G. L. B.

JOHN BULL AND THE GALLIC COCK.*

(1860.)

WHEN Nap the First from Calais shot
  A glance towards our island,
Half envious of Great Britain's lot
  He wished the Channel dry land,
That he, and his, might just run o'er
  Some morn ere day was showing,
And stop the British lion's roar
  With Gallic cocks a-crowing.

    But " Ha ! ha ! ha ! " the waves laughed out,
      To show we did not mind him,
    So Nap he turned his face about
      And clenched his hands behind him.

* Music by W. T. BELCHER; published by J. H JEWELL,
    Great Russell Street, W.C.

When Nap the Third came to the throne,
   How, we'll not stop to mention,
One scheme engrossed his thoughts alone
   (He's clever at invention)—
That was, with Cherbourg forts and guns
   To render unavailing
The pluck of England's naval sons,
   And English ships a-sailing.
      Loud laughed the waves—he heard them not-
        Perhaps they would remind him,
      How Nap the First was "sent to pot,"
        And clenched his hands behind him.

Ten years now flown, and Nap the Third
   Grown strong, and fierce, and haughty,
"John Bull!" screams out the Gallic bird,
   " At last, Old Boy, I've caught ye,
Henceforth the foremost place hold we,
   Our Empire doth unseat ye,"
" By Jove!" says Jack, " ere that shall be
   I'll ring your neck and eat ye! "
      While laugh the Channel waves and say—
        " Old friend Bull, never mind him,
      Let Louis Nap but come your way
        You'll tie his hands behind him! "

WINTER HOURS.

———

Let Spring bring birds and buds,
    Summer its fruits and flowers,
And Autumn tint the woods,
    I love the Winter hours:
The cosy Winter hours, when the blazing fire burns bright,
And friends draw closer round to chat in its ruddy light.

The snow falls thick and fast,
    The frost is on the pane,
And the whistling of the blast,
    Heralds the coming rain—
Yet give me the Winter hours, when brighter shines the fire
And the flame of Friendship's torch, but blazes up the higher.

Isab. B.

NEVERMORE! EVERMORE!

NEVERMORE in hall or street,
  Grove or woodland, bower or glen,
May those ill-starred lovers meet
  As of late they met—again,
        Nevermore! Ah, nevermore!

Nevermore may look or sign,
  Flushing cheek or glancing eye,
Or the earnest written line
  Ask as swift and fond reply.

Nevermore may lip meet lip,
  Or the clasping arms entwine—
Hours like moments by them trip
  To love's music " Mine ! " and " Thine ! "

Nevermore may throbbing heart
Beat against a heart as fond ;
That which rent their lives apart
Sets its seal upon the bond,
Evermore—for evermore!

Evermore Time's sullen stream
Memory's bridge must darkly span,
Trod by shapes from Life's love-dream,
Spectres 'neath the fatal ban.

Ever while the tide of life
Courses through the straining hear
Chafing with its secret strife
Must their pulses beat apart.

Ever each in lonely mood,
Hiding all from stranger eyes,
On the past must inly brood—
Only masked against surprise.

Evermore through weary years,
  Loveless future, life a blot,
Aching heart and frozen tears
  Must be each one's bitter lot.

Oh! the madness of the thought,
  Ringing ever through the brain,
Nevermore may love be sought,
  Evermore we love in vain!
        Nevermore! Evermore!

ISAB. B.

GOOD WE MIGHT DO.

———

Wᴇ all might do good
   Where we often do ill,
There is always the way,
   If we have but the will;
If it be but a word
   Kindly breath'd or suppress'd,
It may ward off some pain,
   Or give peace to some breast.

We all might do good
   In a thousand small ways—
In forbearing to flatter,
   Yet yielding due praise—

In spurning ill rumour,
  Reproving wrong done,
And treating but kindly
  The hearts we have won.

We all might do good,
  Whether lowly or great;
Good deeds are not gauged
  By the purse or estate;
If it be but a cup
  Of cold water that's given,
Like the widow's two mites,
  It is something for heaven.

G. L. B.

A MOTHER'S VOICE.*

I love to hear the mountain rill
 Go singing on its way—
To hear the little skylark trill
 Its spiritual lay—
To list the cooing of the dove,
Or zephyr sighing through the grove
 Towards the close of day ;
But there's a sweeter music still
Than's breathed by skylark, dove, or rill.

I love to hear the glowing tongue
 When old friends meet again—
To hear the lover warm and young,
 Breathe the impassioned strain :—

* Music by W. T. Belcher; published by J. H. Jewell, Great Russell Street.

The words of sister or of wife,
As honied drops can sweeten life,
  And banish half our pain;
But there's a music can transcend
The words of sister, lover, friend.

I heard it first in childhood's years,
  'Ere yet the playful boy
Had drank of grief, or dreamt of tears
  Drawn from the fount of joy;
It is not now, and I deplore
That I can never hear it more—
  That time should e'er destroy
What best can make the heart rejoice,
The music of a Mother's Voice.

                             G. L. B.

THE HAUNTED TOWER.

(NORTH ROAD, DURHAM.)

AYE haunted ! not as legends say,
　　By spectres robed in white ;
No sheeted-ghost glides through the gloom
　　The timid soul to fright.

No elf-light hovers round the pool,
　　Or o er the waterfall,
Nor hath the hooting owl been see
　　Upon the ivied wall.

A solitary bat may flit
　　Athwart the twilight dim,
And wild winds stir the darkening woods
　　With their mysterious hymn.

Yet hath the lofty pine no voice,
　The spreading oak no tale
Of ghastly sight or murderous deed
　Beneath the moonlight pale.

The turret hides no skeleton,
　The vault no rustling chain,
Yet the lone tower is haunted,
　And haunted must remain.

No raven from the battlement,
　Ill omened, croaks of doom ;
Yet there's a shadow on the tower—
　The shadow of the tomb.

'Twas haunted one long summer through
　By two fair gleesome boys,
And tower and woodland rang again
　With buoyant childhood's noise.
　　　　　K 2

But Winter, in his gloomy car,
　　Brought unrelenting Death,
To grasp my brave one's little throat,
　　And stop his pulse and breath.

So swift, so sure the fatal clasp,
　　Skill lost its power to save—
Our noble-hearted boy was gone,
　　Gone to an early grave!

Yet still I hear his ringing voice,
　　His light foot's manly tread;
Ah me! the Tower *is* haunted
　　With the memory of the dead!

Isab. B.

SERVICES AND REWARDS.

Written in aid of the Sir Hugh Myddelton Life Boat Fund, and
spoken by Mrs. F. R. Phillips, 1864.

THIS question stirs my brain, in thoughtful mood,
Who are the wise, the noble, and the good?
There are, who drive th' ensanguined trade of war
And pluck their laurels from proud fields afar;
There are, who sit in senates and control
A nation's action and a nation's soul;
Others, again, in kingly power rejoice—
The gift of conquest, or a people's choice:
Where man's true interests are understood,
All these are wise, are noble, and are good.

The sons of science, heroes of the pen,
Bards, prophets, sages, wonder-working men,

Who bridge our seas, and over mountains lay
Their iron rails to form a world's highway—
Are not these wise, are not these noble, too ?
The age cries, " Yes," and so, I'm sure, will you.
To them a mighty debt of thanks we owe,
Who, strong in faith, strong in endeavour grow—
Who help us cheerly life's rough path along,
And tune our lips to strains of hopeful song.

Once more !   Where victors bare no crimsoned sword,
Nor genius strives, nor spirit-stirring word
Is breathed by lips inspired, there are who plan
The noblest works of charity for man.
See yonder lofty pile, where halt, lame, blind,
Shunned by the crowd, a welcome refuge find ;
See yonder fire brigade, at duty's call,
Mount where flames leap, and burning rafters fall ;
Or, mark again, yon brave devoted band
Put out to sea, with danger near at hand.

God bless our Life Boat crews ! of all who test
Man's boundless love for man, the first and best.

When night winds roar, and angry billows leap
With awful yell from out the yawning deep;
When ships go down, and drowning seamen cry
With piteous wail for " help " that seems not nigh—
Forth from their homes, with martyr-zeal they pour,
Fly to their boats, and quit the treacherous shore;
Thankful at heart if privileged to save
The sire or husband from a watery grave.

To kings and rulers states will statues raise—
For chiefs and statesmen twine the laurel bays—
Give rank, and place, and power to *men* who feign
The patriot's part for their own end and gain;
But what of these true, lion-hearted ones,
The very pink of England's chosen sons!
Whence their reward? Whence theirs! In that great day,
When earth's poor pomp and pride shall pass away,
Of those to whom rich recompence is given
They shall not lack the golden gifts of Heaven.

Meanwhile, 'tis ours to plead their holy cause,
And ask your succour, as the best applause.

Let your warm sympathies the means provide
To launch another Life Boat on the tide;
Arm for stern conflict with the deadly foam
Those gallant men who bring the shipwrecked home :
And, as the mercy-bark rides o'er the surge,
With shouts of joy, where else had swelled a dirge;
So from her chamber dim, the lone wife's prayers
Shall rise above your pillows unawares.

G. L. B.

WOULDST THOU BE A CHILD AGAIN?

" WOULDST thou not fain recall thy childhood's hours,
If wishing would avail ? " was asked of one
Whose sun of life was on the rapid wane.
" Dost thou not sigh for bygone happiness,—
For childhood's pastimes, playmates, innocence,—
Its pure delights, its pleasures unalloyed,—
Its host of joyous fancies, laughing mirth,
And sinless revels; not an anxious thought
To cloud the passing hour with the 'to come: '—
Dost thou not mourn for these, thy friends of old ? "

" Were this a perfect picture, I might wish
Childhood's return,—for mine was sunny, bright,
And its remembrance in my aged heart
Yet dwells serenely, like the rich perfume
That lingers round the dying rose, and from
Each pore distils fresh fragrance, e'en in death.

Bright though it was, I wish not its recall—
Childhood hath sorrows, and, though less acute
Than those of later life, its petty griefs
Most poignant then appear.   Time will not pause ;—
The child *must* progress onward unto age.
My lot has been to mingle with the world,—
A busy dweller among busy men.
How could I wish to tread again the path
Which I have trod, beset with latent snares
And specious joys, that lure but to destroy :
Or cast adrift in childhood's puny bark,
Brave the bleak storms of life's tempestuous sea :
Con o'er again the lessons I have learned
In the sad school of grave experience :
Tempted again, to be again beguiled
By gilded folly's artificial smiles,
The tinsel glitter of a gay outside :
Whirl in the vortex of a giddy crowd,
And, swallowing with rash avidity,
The deadly poison-draught of flattery,
Become the prey of some designing knave :
As years mature the mind, to lose the truth,
The innocence of childhood,—to become
Well versed in worldly cunning, worldly lore,—

When others plot, to counterplot,—to be
A seeker after treasure, honour, fame,
Till coming age reveals their emptiness,
And shows that 'all is vanity?'   Ah, no!
I would not be an unsuspecting child."

    The old man paused ; the querist thus resumed :—
" Hast thou *no* wish to be a child again,
If age could give its wisdom to the child,
Its gravity and sage experience ?
Then 'gainst the tempter's wiles might'st thou be proof,
And, having learned to navigate life's sea,
Pilot thy bark in safety 'mong its rocks,
Its hidden shoals and quicksands.   Knowing well
False pleasure from the true, thou might'st enjoy
The true with greater zest ; and, being skilled
In worldly artifice, shun every snare,
And joyously pursue thy onward way
In undisturbed repose."

                        " Not so, not so ;
Suspicion banishes repose.   The sleep
Of childhood should be calm, serene, and still

A knowledge of the world would rest dispel,
And manhood cast its fetters round the child.
The gladsome frolic wild must be suppressed,
Because, forsooth, it might disaster cause
At some far distant time:—the child must check
Its best affections—they, perchance, might prove
A source of future sorrow, and the friend
The child's warm heart already loves, must be
Held at a distance, lest in future years
He prove unfaithful, and betray his trust.
Nature and knowledge thus at variance,
Where would be childhood's happiness ?   Nature
Would prompt to generous deeds, quick impulses,
Kind sympathies ; knowledge would interpose,—
Chill the *child's heart* with its Medusa's *head*,
And check each liberal feeling with mistrust.
A baby face wearing a careworn brow,—
A childish figure with an old man's heart,
Would be unparalleled anomalies :—
Oh, no ! I would not be an aged child."

He ceased ; again the questioner began : —
"How is it that an old, old man like thee,—

Decrepit, feeble, tottering on the brink
Of Death's steep precipice,—for whom the grave
Already opes its yawning portals wide
To close them o'er thy clay,—whose coil of life
The Fates have spun to a mere filmy thread,
A breath would utterly destroy,—can thus
Serenely contemplate thy coming end ;
And, rather than re-live thy life, prefer
To meet with smiles the enemy of man ? "

" Why should I frown at the approach of Death ?
He has been long expected ; and his home,
The body's sepulchre, encloses not
The never-dying soul   The dreamless tomb
Is but a resting-place 'twixt life and life,
In which the spirit leaves the chrysalis,—
The earthy mass that clogged its flight so long,
And checked its aspirations after home.
Why should I seek to live my life again ?
Ask the long-absent, weary wanderer,
Returning to the haven of his rest,
If, with his own loved home in sight, he would
Relinquish willingly his cherished hopes,

To travel o'er again the same rough road—
His home as yet unwon?   He answers, 'No;
My sad heart yearns for home.'   And shall I be
Less anxious after my eternal rest,
The soul's celestial home, that I should wish
To tread again, a weeping denizen,
The pilgrimage of this embittered world,
When, fainting, I have almost reached the goal?
It may not be!   When thou, young one, hast lived
To note the follies of mankind,—to see
The frailties of the best-spent life,—the care,
The anguish that oft chafes and goads the heart
Of the most joyous, happiest of men;—
Then ponder o'er my words, and ask *thy* heart
If *thou* would'st wish to be a child again?"

ISAB. B.

A WORD FOR THE WORKERS.

<hr>

(THE LANCASHIRE COTTON FAMINE.)

<hr>

WHO'LL lend a hand
To the toilers of the land,
To the brave and gallant band
 Who have made our country great?
From whose faithful labour springs
Wreaths for victors, crowns for kings,
And all world-ennobling things
 That may make a country great.

Who'll lend a hand?
There's sorrow in the land,
O, a sorrow deep and grand
 As the rolling of the years;

Stalwart toilers bow the head,
Hearts are breaking, tears are shed—
Give them succour, give them bread,
    Stem the current of their tears!

Who'll lend a hand
For the honour of our land,
To preserve the noble band
    Who respect their country's laws?
Who look famine in the face,
At their firesides give it place,   `
Yet bring no foul disgrace
    On a starving people's cause.

Who'll lend a hand?
Loom and shuttle idle stand,
Willing workers idle stand,
    Martyr's to a bloody strife;
Till the red stream out is run,
Till "the battle's lost and won,"
North and South again made one,
    Who will feed the Lamp of Life?

                                 G. L. B.

THE MINSTREL OLD AND GREY.

———

An aged Minstrel sat him down
   Beneath the autumn sun,
To wake a well remembered theme,
   Ere life's last sands were run;
Feeble and palsied was his hand,
   His bare head silv'ry grey—
And thus, with trembling voice and tears,
   He sang his plaintive lay:

" Ah! happy once this heart of mine,
   When youth's sun shone for me,
And hope's voice in a whisper came
   Replete with melody;
Life, life was then a holy thing,
   Smiles lit its every day: "
But here the Minstrel's voice grew faint
   With—" now I'm old and grey."

L

Again, the Minstrel struck his harp,
  To sing of manhood's days,
When sweet thought tells how love has birth
  But not how it decays;
Yet while, in mem'ry, to those hours
  His spirit fain would stray,
The chords he touched more plainly told
  That he was old and grey.

Of Friendship's truth he would have sung,
  But strength began to fail,
And chill winds beat around his brow,
  As 'twere, to hush the tale;
Of *all* who loved, not *one* remained
  To gladden life's lone way;
The harp fell from the Minstrel's hand—
  The Minstrel old and grey.

G. L. B.

THE GIPSY GIRL.

— —

*On an exquisite Crayon Drawing, by C. Burlison, Esq., of a Gipsy
Girl, with a burdock-leaf parasol.*

— —

A WITCHING face,

A form of grace,

And an eye of wondrous power,

A rosy lip

A bee might sip

Are thine—thy maiden dower;

Greeting our souls like a glad surprise

Thou Gipsy Girl with the lustrous eyes.

Fair rustic queen,

Thy burdock green

Is a sceptre meet for thee,

Whose greatest spell,

Sweet woodland belle!

Is thy arch simplicity;

But many a maid in halls of state
Might barter wealth for a charm as great.

A winsome thing
In life's young spring
Thou'rt budding, a forest flower :
Oh ! be it thine
Still pure to shine
In life's maturer hour ;
For the glance that beams 'neath that burdock leaf,
Should never be dimmed by guile or grief.

ISAB. B.

UNREAD LESSONS.

———

Dumb stones, 'tis said, can lessons teach,
　　The truths of Heaven revealing,
And " running brooks " divinely preach
　　To mortal sense and feeling ;
But human hearts as soon as born,
　　To folly's dictates leaning,
Will coldly turn away and scorn
　　Their words of sober meaning.

So, in the crowded street we find
　　'Neath pale and unwashed faces,
Of will subdued, and lofty mind,
　　The purest, grandest traces :

But men who plot for worldly gains,
  With baser things confound them—
They cannot see the ore's bright veins
  For dross that lies around them.

One half the blessings hourly sent,
  In mercy, love, and kindness,
To make our stubborn hearts relent,
  And cure our moral blindness,
We cannot, or we will not prize ;
  Like shadows they flit o'er us.
Let's hope they'll not hereafter rise
  In judgment deep before us !

                              G. L. B.

THE STATE PILOT!*

———— ʹ

Of prompt and shrewd State pilots,
   Who knew their country's coast,
The log-book of Old England
   We know can proudly boast;
We pride ourselves on Chatham,
   On Canning, Pitt, and Peel,
And others who have grasped the helm,
   To serve the common weal;
But, while the Dead we honour,
   Some homage let us pay
To England's living Pilot,
   The glory of his day!

* Music by Van Heddigham.

O, Palmerston for England !
   Our flag by him unfurled
May boldly bid defiance
   To the tempests of the World !

In time of doubt and danger,
   When breakers are a head,
To peril the dear liberties
   For which our fathers bled ;
Or when the war-wave threatens
   Around our Isle to sweep,
And stay the power of England
   At home, or on the deep—
There ne'er was such a Pilot
   To mount the quarter-deck,
And guide the old State vessel
   Safe home, 'mid storm and wreck !

O, Palmerston for England !
   Our flag by him unfurled,
May boldly bid defiance
   To the tempests of the World !

G. L. B.

LABOUR'S PROGRESS AND TRIUMPH.

———

Spoken by Mr. Henry Marston at a Benefit Performance in aid of the "London Tin-plate Workers' Pension Fund."

———

WHEN the Phœnicians, guided by the stars,
Made themselves great by commerce, slighting Mars,
And from the shore where Tyrian summer smiles
Steered through the Great Sea's labyrinthine isles,
Passed the rock pillars reared by Hercules,
Row'd through Atlantic's foam to Britain's seas;
They from their galleys leapt on Cornish soil,
Not like a Cæsar, bent on bloody spoil,
But, with indomitable will and zeal,
Forced the dull earth her treasures to reveal;
And, richer far for the bright ore they found,
Made England great as Labour's vantage ground:

Then—the swart miner labouring was a slave,
Dug for his master wealth—himself a grave.

Later, when Roman legions trod the land,
A conquered people laboured at command.
For general good the victors made them toil,
And harvests waved above the new-till'd soil ;
Forts rose, and roads—those great arterial veins
Of a great country—crossed hills, woods, and plains.
For tools and weapons still our mines were wrought,
And what he knew the warlike Roman taught ;
Stamped the imperial seal on wax-like land,
But ground to dust the worker's horny hand.

Successive rulers through contentious years
Deluged our Isle with blood—baptised with tears ;
And Norman William grasp'd with grip of steel
At Saxon freedom, crushed it 'neath his heel ;
With serfdom's fetters bound the groaning mass,
And collar'd, like to hounds, the working class.
They had no rights, by *law*, to life or love,
Might work and wed, rear slaves, but not improve,

Not earn to garner up a thrifty store;
Oppressed and ignorant, they drudged, and *bore!*

But feudalism, in its turn, decayed
Before advancing wants—advancing trade.
While greater despots, ruling other lands,
Drove forth *their* thinking workers in strong bands;
Men, who self-exiled through their strength of will
Or dauntless purpose, men of art and skill,.
.Who flying hither, each with some new craft,
Flourish'd and throve, a healthy, fruitful graft.
But still the humble artizan who wrought
Was cramped and fettered in his act or thought;
Was housed, and clothed, and fed beneath a ban—
Restrained from all that elevates the man.

But as Time's scythe mowed down each kingly race,
Fresh generations took each other's place;
Despots and tyrant-laws died out perforce;
Science and progress kept their onward course;
Men learned to think, and thinking men are strong
To battle for the Right, and hew down Wrong;

And working men upreared their heads at length
With the new power of mind and moral strength;
Conscious that labour dignifies the hand,
And working intellect upholds our land.

Oppression's star has set, and men are free
To work and live in calm security,
They work in hope, and if with sweat-dew'd brow,
Still mine, or forge, or lathe, or loom, or plough,
Holds willing workers, men with hearths and homes
Free as themselves, where no intruder comes;
Where household comforts, not withheld by law,
Cluster around—such serfdom never saw;
Where the lithe infant and the weak old man
Disport together, as such children can;
Where, if a prudent matron guide the store,
The workman's savings grow to more and more.

In times gone by such things could never be,
Manhood might work, but age brought poverty;
Rapacious rulers kept the poor man down,
Alike in country as in fœtid town.

No banks, no clubs, where providence or thrift
Might hoard its savings lest age ran adrift;
The alms-house and the hospital alone
Open'd their doors when manhood's strength was gone.
But self-dependence had not then been taught,
It came with Freedom, and remained with Thought.

To-night you meet to show what Time has done,
How virtues flourish under Freedom's sun;
How prudence and benevolence may blend,
And self-support provide for each old friend;
How honest workers, in their manhood's prime,
May blunt the scythe and clip the wings of Time.
And free to work, to trade, to spend or spare,
You have made age your own peculiar care:
A noble task, for aid so nobly given,
Must rise like incense to the throne of Heaven.

ISAB. B.

THE THREE BLACK D'S.

———

Listen, Friend! Good words are these—
Beware, beware of the three black D's!
And you'll never have cause to repine
That you took this advice of mine:
I have travelled the world for years,
Seen much of its smiles and tears,
And I know, with Drinking, Debt, or Disgrace,
You cannot look the world in the face!

I once knew a tradesman young,
With a sense of right and wrong,
A prospect fair, a placid brow—
Ah! where is that tradesman now?

Drinking robbed him of health,

Beggary came by stealth,

Friends forsook him—hard his case ;

He couldn't look the world in the face!

I once knew a holy man,

To do good was his plan ;

The sick he tended, fed the poor,

And thought himself secure,

Till he borrowed a five pound note—

Till he went in Debt for a coat ;

Debt brought duns, and duns gave chase—

He couldn't look the world in the face !

I once knew a maiden fair

Who had suitors everywhere,

And one she loved too well !

Betrayed by him, she fell ;

Fell in her golden prime—

Fell into secret crime ;

An awful death, to avoid Disgrace—

She couldn't look the world in the face !

Listen, Friend! goods words are these,
Beware, beware of the three black D's!
They are monsters in disguise—
They are flatterers breathing lies—
They speak you fair, they mean you ill,
The body will ruin, the soul will kill;
Resist their wiles, Disgrace, Drink, Debt—
The Devil's black art alphabet!

                                        G. L. B.

THE QUIET JOYS OF HOME. *

———

GIVE me the quiet joys of home,
  The peace that passeth outward show,
And let who will contentless roam
  In quest of joys he ne'er may know;
A heart to love, a friend to cheer,
  A smiling hearth, and more beside,
A hand to chase away the tear
  And soothe the soul when sorrow-tried;
Give me but these, I ask no more,
With them I'm rich, without them poor.

•

Give me the quiet joys of home,
  And I will shun ambition's way—
The seat of power, the courtly dome,
  And all that tempts to lead astray;

* Music by CHARLES BERNARD.

M

My children sitting on my knee,
The household faces gathered round,
Are sweeter, dearer, far to me
Than aught else in the world I've found;
Give me but these, I ask no more,
With them I'm rich, without them poor.

G. L. B.

DESOLATION.

Alone, alone, ever alone!
At morn, and noon, and night,
When tears will start she may not own,
Nor shed save out of sight;
Alone with her weary load of care,
Alone should a joy bird sing,
But the fleeting joys which none may share
Depart on a rapid wing.

Alone, alone, ever alone!
In the daily walk of life,
Her fears, and hopes, and aims unknown,
Lonely, and yet a wife!

M 2

Alone, her watch by the sufferer's bed,
   Alone when she kneels in prayer,
Alone when she weeps o'er each buried head,
   With none in her grief to share.

Alone, alone, ever alone!
   Hers is that dreary lot,
Loving—to long for the love unshown,
   Living—a life forgot;
Feeling the spirit within rebel,
   Yet crushing rebellion down,
Lest an angry word to the lip should swell,
   Or the forehead learn to frown.

Alone, alone, ever alone!
   She weaves her web of thought,
All unheeded and all unknown,
   Yet thus a shroud is wrought;
For slowly and sadly day by day,
   As water-drops wear the stone,
This thought rings the knell of her life alway—
   " Alone, for ever alone!"

                    Isab. B.

BETTER THINGS SHALL COME TO PASS.

BETTER things shall come to pass—
    When the reign of pride shall cease
    Throughout the world,
    When the rule of selfishness
    Is downward hurled,
    When the light of knowledge shines
    In every heart,
And the clouds of prejudice
    Thrown back, depart :—
      Then, may men look up again,
      And behold, as in a glass,
      This inspiring truth revealed—
      Better things have come to pass !

Better things shall come to pass—
 When to man his fellow man
  Shall kindly turn,
 When the flame of mutual love
  Shall brightly burn,
 When might's fetter by its light
  Shall be riven,
 And the warring mind becomes
  More like heaven :—
   Then, may men look up again,
    And behold, as in a glass,
   This inspiring truth revealed—
    Better things have come to pass !

Better things shall come to pass—
 When the weak become the strong,
  Aye, strong in truth ;
 When the old retain the faith,
  They held in youth ;
 When the wilful blind shall see,
  Each face to face,
 And the bitterest foes are clasped
  In warm embrace:—

Then, may men look up again,
And behold, as in a glass,
This inspiring truth revealed—
Better things have come to pass !

Better things shall come to pass—
When the happiness of all,
And not the few,
Leads the great ones of the earth
To think and do ;
When our prisons vainly wait
To strengthen crime,
And the last in pauper walls
Has spent his time:—
Then, may men look up again,
And behold, as in a glass,
This inspiring truth revealed—
Better things have come to pass !

Better things shall come to pass—
When the law of Love prevails
O'er all the earth,

When justice and forbearance
　　Spring to birth,
When men shall strive together,
　　And contend
O'er power, o'er hate, and fear,
　　For life's great end:—
　　　Then may men look up again,
　　　And behold, as in a glass,
　　　This inspiring truth revealed—
　　　Better things have come to pass!

G. L. B.

PARTING WORDS.

———

I DEEMED thy words might be believed,
   That they were born of love and truth ;
But time has shown I was deceived,
   Thy vows are valueless forsooth.

Had thine been love to bide the blast,
   To bid temptation stand aside,
I could have loved thee to the last,
   Howe'er the world that love had tried.

But false and fickle, go thy way!
   Flutter from flower to flower awhile,
Forgetful that night follows day,
   That skies may frown as well as smile.

How deep soe'er a woman's love,
    A woman's pride is deeper still,
And rising far thy loss above
    I'll conquer love by strength of will.

Yet, when all radiant with glee,
    With present bliss and love elate,
Deep in the cells of memory
    The past my form will reinstate.

Thou canst not drive the image back ;
    Thou canst not blot the record plain :
Love travels not without a track,
    And memory lives for joy or pain.

Then, since thy love no more be mine,
    And thou inconstant art to me,
Woo where thou wilt, nor think I pine—
    I loved when loved—so thou art free!

                                        Isab. B.

THE MEN OF OLD.

We sometimes sneer at ancient days,
    And blame the men of old,
Who listened to the simple lays
    By Saxon gleemen told ;
We wonder at the lives they led,
With no grand prospects overhead.

Because no railway ploughed the land,
    No steamer rode the main,
We deem them a benighted band,
    Who lived and toiled in vain.
No books had they—no press—no pen,
And so we call them slaves, not men !

Methinks to that old time and race
   A mighty debt we owe,
Who freedom won, with sweating face,
   A thousand years ago ;
Who laid a glory that should last
In deep foundations of the past.

Their lives were rude, their wants were few,
   They had no vain desires ;
But never men more brave and true
   Than those heroic sires,
The fathers through a thousand years,
Of England's noble volunteers !

                                     G. L. B.

HOUSEHOLD TREASURES.

———

A pleasant sound is in my home,
  Throughout the household ringing clear,
As 'twere a spirit-voice had come
  A parent's anxious heart to cheer;
From morn till night that sound is heard,
Sweet as the song of summer bird.

A gladsome smile is in my home,
  Lights up the room in which I sit,
And half the day o'er sunbeams come
  And through the window peep at it;
From early morn till close of day
That smile illumes life's cloudy way.

God bless young children! who make home,
  With all its cares, a paradise—
Who, sinless as the angels, come
  To woo us with their heavenly eyes;
God bless young children! whom we're told,
The world's Redeemer blest of old.

                                        G. L. B.

JOAN D'ARC.

RAPT Joan! visionary maid,
   What frenzy fires thy soul?
What projects seethe within thy brain,
   Spurning the mind's control;
That thou, an untaught peasant girl,
   With madness in thy glance,
Unaided, and alone, should'st frame
   Thy plans to rescue France?
Hath Heaven indeed appointed thee
To set thy captive country free?

Wild Joan! strong must be the spell
   To banish from thy face,
The virgin bashfulness that aye
   Is woman's fairest grace.

But stronger still must be the spell,
    Empowering thee to hold
Thine influence o'er the minds of men,
    Sage priests, or warriors bold,
And cause a King and Court to bend
Lowly to thee, their hope and friend.

Brave Joan ! girt with mystic sword,
    And armed from head to heel,
Thy charger bears thee proudly on
    To guard thy country's weal.
No doubts delay thy mission now,
    The foe quails at thy name,
On ! thou hast promised victory,
    Go, and that victory claim.
The warlike Maid hath won the day,
Onward to Rheims—away, away !

Proud Joan ! prelates, nobles, king,
    All render thanks to thee ;
The Prophetess redeems her pledge,
    Charles bends the Royal knee ;
And she, a country servant girl
    Anoints and crowns a King ;

Sharing the homage of the crowd
  Who of her valour sing.
Joan ! this is thy hour of pride :—
Ruling the rulers at thy side !

Famed Joan ! bright is thy career,
  But brief as it is bright,
A meteor's transitory ray
  Athwart the darksome night !
For treachery, with its poisoned fang,
  Hath marked thee for its prey,
And foes without, and foes within,
  Have limited thy sway.
The city yields—she fights alone :—
Vain 'gainst their hosts the arm of one !

Lost Joan ! prisoner tho' thou art,
  Thy brow is yet serene ;
Firm and intrepid as thy life,
  So is thy closing scene.
Deserted in thy utmost need
  By every earthly friend,
The power who strengthened thee before
  Supports thee to the end.

N

Nor stake, nor pile, can make thee yield,
The God of Daniel is thy shield.

Poor Joan! Saviour thou of France!
    How art thou now repaid?
A painful, ignominious death
    Is thine, grand Orleans Maid.
And those, who hailed thee Saint erewhile,
    Brand thee a Sorceress now.
Unfortunate! the *shame* was *theirs*:—
    A glorious patriot thou!
Laurel-and-fame-wreathed thou shalt be,
Thy country's immortality.

ISAB. B.

SLANDER!

" 𝕿𝖍𝖔𝖚 𝖘𝖍𝖆𝖑𝖙 𝖓𝖔𝖙 𝖇𝖊𝖆𝖗 𝖋𝖆𝖑𝖘𝖊 𝖜𝖎𝖙𝖓𝖊𝖘𝖘 𝖆𝖌𝖆𝖎𝖓𝖘𝖙 𝖙𝖍𝖞 𝖓𝖊𝖎𝖌𝖍𝖇𝖔𝖚𝖗! '

Of all the evils that afflict mankind
From Crinoline to Murder, most we find
Slander abound.   Slander! that imp of sin
Which ope's the door to let the Devil in.
In shape Protean, with as many eyes
As Argus had, to look unspoken lies,
It suits itself to every hour and place
Within the compass of the human race;
Speaks every language underneath the sun—
Knows all that is, and all that is not done—
Makes much of ill, and little of the good—
Tells what it should not, and not what it should—

Now dull, now sad, now lively, now severe,
Forcing a laugh, or straining at a tear.
So Slander dogs the round World on its way,
Sowing new crops of misery each day.

Sworn in it service, evil agents twain,
Gossip and Scandal toil with busy brain.
First Gossip, fashioned like a maiden fair,
Or withered spinster, t' whom the tender care
Of love's a stranger, runs its busy round
Of observation.   Eager as a hound
That scents out blood, it travels in one track,
Ne'er stopping short, nor, wearied, turning back
In the pursuit.   The slightest act or word
Quick in its active memory is stored
For future use, with such embellishment
Of thought and inference as shall, when blent,
Produce a startling picture.   Neighbours doors
Half open, furnish incidents by scores
For shrewd surmise, and undrawn curtains let
In furtive glances—glances that shall set
" The table in a roar," and fire pert tongues
With condemnation of conjectured wrongs.

Nor less the skill with which its arts are veiled,
The vain regrets expressed, the sorrow wailed
In tragic accents, liked a player versed
In parts a thousand times or more rehearsed.
Roscius, an actor was of matchless power—
Rome's glory, and the stage's highest dower ;
Kean, Kemble, Garrick, these, too, had their day,
Strutted the " boards" awhile, then passed away ;
But Gossip is their master, through all years
It moves mankind to laughter and to tears.

Close at its heels, bold as a robber chief,
Where Gossip falters, Scandal brings relief.
Scandal !   Behold it at the Counter stand,
With scales and weights (short weights) in either hand,
Doling out goods adulterate—sloe-leaf tea,
Horse-bean rich mocha, whiting flour, "P. D."—
List'ning with eager ears to what may drop
From frequent callers at the " Gossip shop."
Here Susan Mangle cites her tale of grief—
Here Lawyer Ferret reads his lying brief—
Here Vestrydom expounds its little schemes,
And, flushed with hope, of future triumph dreams ;

Here drivelling Cant, and Prejudice, and Fraud
Concert together, and themselves applaud;
Here plot propounds, and daring executes—
One tips the arrow, and another shoots;
Here friend on friend in treacherous judgment sits,
And dolts and dullards point the shaft at wits;
Here passions rage, "like devils in their pain,"
And fillips smite the cheek without a stain.

That night, while teacups clatter at the board,
And clubs and cliques unite in foul discord—
While neighbour B. to neighbour C. gives ear,
And ribald tongues at sad misfortune jeer,
The mischief spreads.   Hints, winks, and nods give place
To grim surmises, accusations base,
Loud-voiced reproof, and threats.   Next day, and next,
The self-same preaching, from the self-same text,
Continues.   Mischief spreads; like lightning flies
From house to house, and town to town—defies
Both time and distance, till a hundred lands
Listen aghast with uplift eyes and hands.
Even as acorns turn to giant trees,
And little rills to rivers vast, and seas;

So Scandal gathers—gathers as it goes,
From doubtful harm, to worst of human woes,
And what at first was but a trivial thing
May banish princes or depose a king.

Alas! that men will serve this hateful fiend—
Professing Christian men—themselves not screened
From its attacks.   Down on their knees they pray
" Forgive our trespasses," and go straightway
And brew a scandal base, as though fair fame
Was meant to be a mark for venomed aim.
Pull down our churches, lay our chapels low,
If those who fill their cushioned seats will grow
In foul hypocrisy, and give the lie
To Him who taught us Christian charity!
A faith of words, and not a faith of deeds,
Is worse than Pagan forms and Pagan creeds,
Which still mean something—symbolize a thought,
Rudely perceived, and hence but rudely taught.
The wild-cat will not prey upon its kind—
E'en here the nobler human lags behind;
The beast instructs the Christian—man, poor man,
How art thou fallen in great Nature's plan!

O, Slander ! Slander ! vilest fiend of hell !
By which the patriarchal Doge erst fell ;
Which poisoned Socrates, and madly hurled
Its shafts at him who sought the Western World ;
Which struck the gentle Flora Hastings down
Beneath the shadow of the British crown ;
Which counts its victims hourly by the score,
Yet seeks, and shrieks, and raves, and gasps for more.
Where'er men turn they meet thee, noisome pest !
Crawling about God's earth in wild unrest;
Now chasing from the pillowed head repose—
Now changing trusty friends to bitter foes—
Anon embarking in ensanguined strife,
Unbarring Death's dark gates to let out Life.

Yon hopeless bankrupt, spurned by passers by—
Yon ruined outcast, breathing forth a sigh—
Yon frenzied maniac, lost to time and sense—
Yon suicide, heart-broken, rushing hence—
Yon duellist intent on scenes of blood—
These, and a thousand others in like mood,
Are thine, O Slander ! Where thy fangs take hold
Each genial current freezes, hearts grow cold

As Polar ice, and lips to mercy sworn,
Breathe only hatred, violence, and scorn.

Above the pomp, and pride, and glare of things,
The laws of rulers, and the power of kings ;
Above the flights of genius, and the light
Of sword-blades flashing in victorious fight ;
Above the patriot's cause, the martyr's crown,
Soars human Honour, heavenward; strike it down,
Debase, disfigure it, and dispossess't
Of all that gave it welcome to the breast,
The spirit pines to death.   No second grace,
Can yield its gifts, or occupy its place.
It is the very jewel of the mind,
Set in a workmanship of gold, refined
By fire Promethean.   When Adam ate
The fruit forbidden in his first estate,
And ruined seized his peace, one glittering star
Through Eden's closing portals shone afar
Into the future—cursed, condemned, disdained,
The hope of Honour still to him remained—
Cheered his dull footsteps through the coming gloom
And kindled rays of glory round the tomb.

The ancient laws of men were framed to guard
This sov'ran virtue—its own rich reward !
Death was the punishment that marked a lie.
In modern codes less stringent rules apply.
Slander is licensed by the world's consent,
And put in force by minds on evil bent.
'Tis time to preach anew the olden truth,
In years of age, of sanctity, of youth—
" Bear not false witness ! " Speak well or be dumb—
Who judges here, is judged in life to come !

G L. B.

MY DEAD BABE'S HAIR.

Thou art laid within the grave, my boy,
　My beautiful and fair,
And all that now remains of thee
　Is this soft lock of hair.
When the shroud was folded round thee,
　'Twas severed from thy head :
Now, tearfully I gaze on it,
　And wish thou wert not dead.
Yet I do wrong to grieve for thee,
　Thou art an angel now,
And brighter than this relic
　Is the glory round thy brow.

Thy upturned eye, and folded hands,
　Folded as if in prayer,
Oft made me pause in reverence,
　I felt the angel there.

In love and awe I kissed thy brow,
  And clasped thee to my breast,
Thinking to keep thee ever there,
  And lull thee so to rest.
But I do wrong to grieve for thee,
  Thou art an angel now,
And brighter than this relic
  Is the glory round thy brow.

I called thee oft a cherub,—ah !
  It came not to my thought,
Thy wings would be so speedily
  Unto perfection brought:
Full fledged they were around thee
  From the moment of thy birth,
. Thou wert from Heaven, and couldst not stay
  A truant here on earth.
And it is wrong to grieve for thee,
  Thou art an angel now,
And brighter than this relic
  Is the glory round thy brow.

                              ISAB. B.

ROUND AND ROUND THE CORAL BOWER.*

(FAIRIES' SONG.)

ROUND and round the coral bower
 Fairies dance the live-long day,
Watchful lest the water's power
 Bear some jutting reef away.
Now they whisper, now they sing
 To the undulating waves,
As their silver voices ring
 Round about the coral caves.

* Music by the Honorable CLEMENTINA FITZWIGRAM; published by CRAMER & Co., Regent Street.

Lo ! they enter and prepare
   For the transports of the night,
Wreathing in their shining hair
   Coral branches snowy white.
Hark ! an echo soft and sweet,
   As they press the sleeping waves,
Makes still music to their feet
   In the silent coral caves.

Once again their hands entwine,
   And the evening banquet spread,
Many a white reef stained with wine
   Like a maiden blushes red.
Now the festal rite is o'er,
   Daylight peeps into the waves,
And the fairies dance once more
   Round about the coral caves.

                G. L. B.

THE GOLDEN CALF.*

The world may sneer and the world may laugh
At those who worship the Golden Calf,
But he has a cure for the wildest jest
Who has taken good care to feather his nest;
Who has thought to himself—" A golden egg
Is better than having to borrow or beg;"
For say what you will, in Life's sunniest day,
There is nothing like gold for the world's highway.

Nothing like gold,

Nothing like gold,

There is nothing like gold for the world's highway.

* Music by STEPHEN GLOVER; published by DUFF AND HODGSON, Oxford Street.

The world may jeer and the world may laugh
At those who worship the Golden Calf,
But wait till the wolf only comes to the door
To reckon the worth of a guinea in store ;
Ha, ha, boys ! 'tis wealth brings us honour and friends,
Should it leave us, O, quickly their friendship ends ;
For say what you will, in life's stormiest day
There is nothing like gold for the world's highway.

      Nothing like gold,
      Nothing like gold,
There is nothing like gold for the world's highway.

        G. L. B.

FANNY'S VALENTINE.

———

Dear Harry, have you quite forgot
  The girl you left behind you!
That it has fallen to my lot
  To write, and thus remind you
A soldier should be brave and *true*,
Not quit an old love for a new?

I fear you have forgotten quite
  The time so bright and sunny,
When I appeared your sole delight,
  And sweeter far than honey;
But well I know that honey cloys,
And men break hearts as children toys,

o

I hear you have another flame
  Whom you intend to marry
But if you have, at once proclaim
  That you are faithless, Harry—
I do not mean to pine and fret,
But wed another, and—forget.

So let me know at once your mind,
  Nor like a booby tarry—
I'll wait for you if you're inclined
  To love me still, dear Harry;
And on this day of Valentine,
Vow to be ever true and thine.

But if, as I begin to think,
  You're an inconstant lover,
Confess—nor fear that I shall shrink
  Your falsehood to discover;
I'll give my heart in fair exchange,
But not to one inclined to range.

ISAB. B.

LION-HEARTED ENGLAND.

A WEE little spot is this island of ours—
    A mere speck on the breast of the ocean ;
Yet it ranks in the world as the grandest of powers—
Its homes are not frowned on from castles and towers,
And the hopes of its sons, pure as incense of flowers,
    Rise on altars of loyal devotion.
'Tis the dread of the despot—the pride of the free,
    And the sun of its glory sets never ;
When its prestige declines, or its ships leave the sea,
        A farewell to freedom for ever !
            For ever
        A farewell to freedom for ever !

There are lands in the east, there are lands in the west,
    Where our laws and our language are written ;
Where the pulse of the Saxon beats warm in each breast,
And the genius of Alfred is proudly impressed

On empires and races that rise to attest,

    How vast are the triumphs of Britain.

Great Britain! the home of the valiant and free,

    The sun of whose glory sets never;

When her prestige declines, or our ships leave the sea,

        A farewell to freedom for ever!

            For ever!

        A farewell to freedom for ever!

The tyrants of earth may unite and propose

    To diminish our might or invade us;

Who cares for their threats, or would shrink from their
    blows,

When the red-lettered page of our history shows

We have risen to power on the necks of our foes,

    That we are what the foeman hath made us?

The scourge of aggression, the shield of the free,

    A nation whose glory sets never;

When our prestige declines, or our ships leave the sea,

        A farewell to freedom for ever!

            For ever!

        A farewell to freedom for ever!

                G. L. B.